Amagansett '84

Cover design and interior maps of Long Island
by Jason Enterline, Enterline Design

Published in the United States by
Gatekeeper Press
7853 Gunn Hwy., Suite 209
Tampa, FL 33626
www.GatekeeperPress.com

Thanks

To the Utah Arts Council for a grant to help get this project started; David Stevenson and David Kranes for closely reading early drafts and for offering encouragement; Tom Hazuka for his sharp eye and eminent good sense as the story continued to take form; Jenny Williams, for graciously reading and re-reading final drafts, offering fresh insight, and helping bring the story to a close.

–SR

Amagansett '84

Shelby Raebeck

gatekeeper press™

Tampa, Florida

In Memory
of my mother, Charlotte
and my oldest sister, Leslie

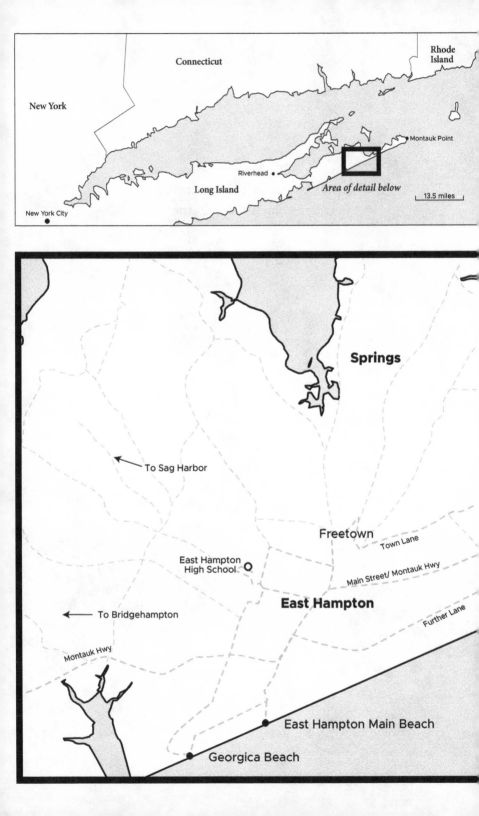

Long Island's East End

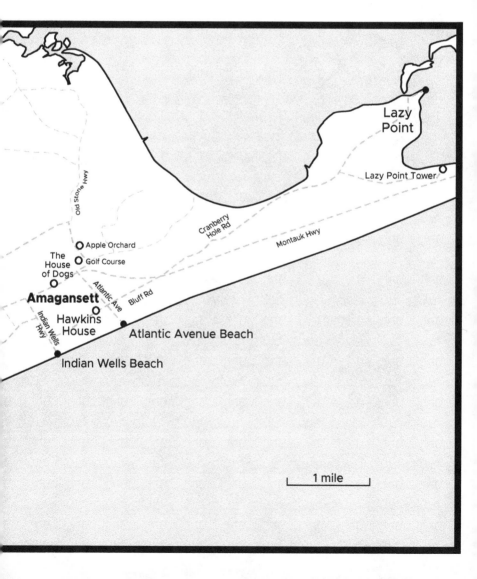

Lazy
Point

Lazy Point Tower

Old Stone Hwy

Cranberry
Hole Rd

Montauk Hwy

Apple Orchard

The
House
of Dogs

Golf Course

Amagansett

Atlantic Ave

Bluff Rd

Indian Wells
Hwy

Hawkins
House

Atlantic Avenue Beach

Indian Wells Beach

1 mile

Chapter 1

MY MOTHER DIED in May 1982, the end of my sophomore year of high school, and though my basketball coach tried to talk him out of it, my father decided to move the four of us—him, my two sisters, and me—full-time to our second home in Amagansett, which was actually our first home. We kids had all been born and begun school in Amagansett, only moving up-island when my dad got promoted to his company's main office in Patchogue.

After a two-week leave, my father resumed work, commuting four days a week, and soon began staying over one night at the home of a woman colleague, then two nights.

As the oldest, Lonnie was the one to feel my father's and, while she'd been alive, my mother's neglect—if that's too strong a word, call it inattention, or distraction—most directly. One of my earliest memories was of Lonnie, ten maybe eleven years old, standing on the back deck insisting she'd just heard somebody trying to break through her bedroom window, my mother and father sitting before her with cocktails, laughing dismissively, assuring her it had only been the wind.

Tessy, at fifteen, was the youngest and took a polarly opposite approach—instead of fighting she turned inward. Already timid, once my mother died, Tessy withdrew further, and her fears in isolation grew stronger.

I was sixteen and floated in a kind of limbo, somewhere in the middle.

⌘

One afternoon in late June, school year over—Tessy and I enrolling but not bothering to attend East Hampton High for the last few weeks of the year—I returned from the beach after watching the Bristers, one of two remaining haul-seining crews. I passed beneath the maples before the ramshackle Victorian fixer-upper Dad and Mom had bought from a fishing family that moved away, the trees having sprouted into thick green masses that tossed in the wind off the ocean.

Inside, my father waved me in to join my sisters who sat on the sofa before him in the living room.

"I want you to know," he said, "I've invited Gladys to join us for the summer."

"It's too soon," Lonnie said.

"Things are different now," my father said, his voice firm, resolved.

"But this is *our* house," Lonnie said. "We all have to decide."

"Lonnie," my father said, "this is not *your* house."

Lonnie exhaled angrily. "Mom would never say that to her children."

"This is not about your mother," my father said.

Lonnie leaned forward. "Why do you want to erase her?" she said.

"I'm doing no such thing," my father said.

"And erase us too," Lonnie said.

My father turned away, giving his head a shake, as if to dislodge the accusation, and walked from the room.

The three of us sat there in silence, Lonnie in the middle staring out, Tessy shifting her eyes from Lonnie down to her clasped hands, then to me, and back to Lonnie.

A simple truth we, like all children, intuitively sensed, was that when it comes to family, if you don't get it right the first time, there's a good chance you never will.

Late that night, I woke up hearing voices and wandered down to the living room as my father was walking out, Lonnie scolding him from the sofa.

"You can't even face me!" she shouted.

My father spun back, pointing a finger at her, and I stepped to the side.

"You will not blame me," he said. "Not for what happened tonight, not for anything." He glared at her another moment and left the room.

I sat in the La-Z-Boy across from Lonnie who drew in several deep breaths. She had been taking him on forever it seemed.

Her eyes locked on mine. "He's afraid of me," she said. "He's a coward."

"Maybe if you eased up a little," I said.

"You mean if I disappeared?"

"I mean if you stopped taking him on."

Lonnie peered over at me. "So I should just roll over and let him lay all this shit on us?"

"I'm just saying, Mom's gone and things have changed."

"Yes," Lonnie said, "*Mom* is gone. We are not."

Tessy trudged into the room in her nightgown and plopped down next to Lonnie.

"What were you arguing about?" I said to Lonnie.

"What's the only reason any of us ever talk to him?" she said.

"Trouble," Tessy said. "What happened?"

"I got a DUI in Carter's car."

"You're still seeing that guy?" I said. "Hasn't it been two weeks?"

"The cops called Dad," Lonnie said, "and he had to come get me and pay two hundred dollars. And you know the first thing he said when we were in the car? 'Where you gonna get the two hundred?'"

Lonnie turned to me. "It wasn't me who started it," she said, her voice raspy and fierce. "It was him. You hear me? *Him.*"

Next morning, I woke to a pelting rain and went straight to Lonnie's room where the closet and dresser drawers were open and empty. Tessy walked in behind me.

"She went to Florida," Tessy said. "Carter got some job down there."

"It's the wrong time of year to go to Florida," I said.

Tessy stood looking at me with watery eyes, lips rolled in. She tried to smile but a sob leaked out, and she stepped over and hugged me. I squeezed her back, hard, trying to anchor her as best I could, and Tessy coughed with a small burst of laughter.

"Can't breathe," she said.

I released my hold and the sadness returned to her face as she stepped toward the window and the view of wet trees lining Bluff Road, with the broad gray backdrop of ocean and sky.

"Maybe it's for the best," I said. "She and Dad aren't ever going to get along."

"But they could," Tessy said, gazing at the still trees beneath the low cover of clouds. "I know they could."

Tessy went back to bed and once the rain let up, I climbed out my bedroom window onto the roof over the front porch. To the east, a pale sun fought its way through the overcast sky, while to the south a thin fog rolled in off the ocean, billowing against the dunes, dissipating before it reached Bluff Road.

The Brister crew—two pickups, the second towing a green dory, a shark's gaping maw with jagged teeth painted on its bow—passed on the street below and turned onto Atlantic Avenue toward the beach.

The trucks stopped at the road's end where a figure slid out of each to switch the hubs to four-wheel-drive, then descended into the sand and faded into the fog. I climbed back through the window, down the two flights of stairs, and walked barefoot to the beach.

I headed toward the faint silhouettes of the pickups and dory a few hundred yards up the shore where the small crew backed the dory, still on the trailer, into the calm ocean. Wesley Brister drove the truck and his two sons, along with a fourth hand I didn't know, all clad in black hip waders, slid the boat off the trailer into the water.

They guided the dory through the small waves, then the two Brister boys climbed in, lowered the outboard motor and headed out, one unloading armfuls of net as the other steered the motor, the dory fading but never disappearing as they carved a gradual arc, out, up a way, and back to the beach.

The fourth guy joined Wesley in the truck and, turning back to meet the dory, Wesley spotted me, rolled down his window.

"Ricky boy," he said.

"How's the fishing?" I said.

"Can't catch what ain't there," he said. "It's a good thing us bubbies is so damn dumb," he added with a wink. "Otherwise, we'd be downright miserable." And he drove off to meet the dory.

Chapter 2

TUCKED BEHIND THE grade school, a square brick building with white Doric columns, the basketball court sat empty, sunny and windless, and I started my afternoon session with a few lay-ups, then shot jumpers from the corner, scooting in after the rebounds, seeing how long I could go without letting the ball touch the court, tossing up a high arcing shot from one corner, running beneath it and grabbing it as it caromed off the rim or fell through the net, and continuing on to the other corner.

After a long string of makes, I noticed Minkoff, an undersized ninth grader, shooting at the other end. His ball nearly as wide as his body, he wore thick, black-rimmed glasses held on with a band. I watched him hoist up a shot and mutter when it missed, then turned back to my hoop and started shooting from the top of the key, following up each miss with a tip-in.

As the sweat started flowing, I found myself getting above the rim, dropping the rebounds down into the basket. Then, completely loose, I bounced the ball hard off the asphalt toward the basket, ran in and jumped, catching the ball before it reached the hoop and throwing it down. The next one I caught and threw down backwards.

"How the hell do you do that?" Minkoff had wandered down to my end.

"I just do it," I said, and dribbled in from the foul line and tomahawked a dunk from behind my head with both hands.

"No," Minkoff said, "*walking* you just do. There's something wrong with you."

Minkoff turned around and ambled back to the other end. When he reached the foul line he sprinted toward the hoop and went up with the ball cocked behind his head as if to dunk, but didn't even bother to release it, the peak of his jump a full two feet below the rim.

"You're too short," I called down, meaning it wasn't that he couldn't jump.

"Very astute," he called back. "Very fucking astute."

༄

One concession my father had made to Tessy was letting her go to a small private school in Bridgehampton, two towns away, with the stipulation that transportation would be up to her. Tessy started out the school year walking each morning to Montauk Highway and hitchhiking to school, then in October began staying overnight at a classmate's house in Bridgehampton, evenings at home growing quiet, Dad and Gladys sitting in the back room reading and watching television.

One November evening I came home in time for steamed vegetables and brown rice, the usual fare since

Dad and Gladys had begun their new diet. I dug some soy sauce out of the cabinet and drenched the food as Dad and Gladys resumed their conversation.

"So we call Ron and we're in?" Gladys said. "Or is there some formal application?"

"Just sponsorship and approval," my father said.

"What's this?" I asked.

"A group called The Sentinels," my father said without lifting his eyes from his plate.

"This fabulous bunch of people," Gladys said, "that believe in a direct link between the natural environment and the human spirit."

"An environmental group?" I said.

"Yes," my father said.

"Their next issue is the aquifer," Gladys said. Then to my father, "We need to get in on this one."

"The what?" I said.

"Aquifer," my father said. "Underground water supply. Rezoning is needed to prevent people from building on it— from building on such small plots."

"The mansions out here," I said, "are built on acres."

"Not them," my father said. "Places like Freetown and Springs. Lazy Point."

"You mean where the locals live," I said.

"Sometimes," Gladys said, "the locals have a hard time looking at the big picture."

Something felt odd about them, transplants from elsewhere, criticizing the locals. Though at least they wanted to preserve the place. I excused myself from the table, pulled on a jacket and gloves, and went out into the dark to find my bike.

On game nights I'd ride to the high school in East Hampton to watch the basketball team. Though I ached to be playing—as a tenth grader at my old school I'd been a varsity starter—since my mother's death and the move back to the East End, I'd been more comfortable on the periphery.

The East Hampton coach yelled constantly from the sideline but Lance Williams, a slender 6' 2" junior from Freetown, the Black section of East Hampton, was the leader on the court. They had other talents, including Wesley Brister's third son, Ben, a deadly long-range shooter, but Lance seemed one step ahead of the rest, jogging up the court, his back to the dribbler, turning back and sliding over at the exact moment the guy passed the ball to intercept it, less a thief than some sort of prophet.

After school I played alone on the court behind the Amagansett school, the winter weather growing too cold even for Minkoff. It rained and sleeted but didn't snow until the first week of March, and I shoveled the heavy snow off the court and kept playing. It wasn't a great deal of fun shooting a cold wet ball, but better than not playing at all, and most days I ended up stripping away layers as I ran up and down the court.

One chilly afternoon in late March, I was down to a T-shirt, running end to end, seeing how many dunks I could make in a row, the first half dozen coming easily before I started straining.

Walking over to pick up the ball, I noticed a blue car, an old Taurus station wagon, at the end of the driveway, and inside a dark figure watching. I took a moment to catch my breath, then dribbled hard to the basket and took off, holding the ball at my hips and whipping it backward over my head, down through the hoop.

A few days later the same blue car pulled in the driveway and Lance Williams got out. He walked over blowing into cupped hands.

"Too cold to be out here," he said. "Lance," he said, offering a hand.

"Ricky," I said.

"Yeah," he said, "I heard there was a backwards-dunking ghost out here. Thought maybe I'd come by and get a game."

"Sure," I said.

Lance peeled off his jacket, took a couple of warm-up shots, and we chose for the ball, Lance winning and moving out to the top of the key.

"Play to eleven?" he said.

"Sure."

The first time he came at me I wasn't prepared for his speed, and he blew past me for an easy basket. Playing make-it-take-it, Lance kept the ball, but this time I cut him off, forcing him to take a jump-shot, which I blocked.

After a see-saw battle, I had the ball, down 10-9. I dribbled once and took a long shot, then, seeing it was going to bounce off the rim, took a running start, leapt over Lance and slammed the ball with one hand through the basket.

Lance broke his game face for the first time, peering at me cock-eyed.

"Where the hell are you from?" he said.

"Here," I said, "Amagansett."

"Alright," he said, "next basket wins."

Tightening his defense, Lance forced me into a bad shot, grabbed the rebound and dribbled out to the key where I met him, crouching low. He backed me toward the basket, took a quick step back, and flicked off a jump-shot before I could leave my feet. I turned and watched the ball fall through the net.

"Good game," he said, offering a hand.

"Yeah," I said.

He picked up his jacket and walked through the gate, the back of his shirt dark with sweat, then turned around and looked at me through the chain-link fence, his breath steaming in the cold air.

"I've seen you in school," he said. "You don't say much."

"Guess not," I said.

"Yeah, well," he said, "sometimes maybe there ain't nothing *to* say."

He gazed at me another moment, nodded, and walked to the car.

Chapter 3

I N APRIL IT rained nearly every day but in May the gray
sky broke apart and the wind washing in off the ocean
began to warm, the maples sprouting into thousands
of tiny buds. Tessy signed up for a home gardening
independent study and started hitching home from school
after lunch. She turned a small plot out back by the shed
with a hoe, and each afternoon when I came home from
school, I'd see her out there planting or weeding.

One of the first warm days, the sky a mild blue with
huge puffs of cloud, I found Tessy leaning on one hand,
pulling weeds with the other, one knee poking her white
dress into a small tent.

"Why you wearing a dress?" I asked.

Tessy looked up, loose strands of blond hair hanging
across her face. "Don't pester," she said, "I'm trying to
think," and she looked back down.

"About what?" I asked.

But she didn't answer, just sat there tugging weeds, so
I headed off to play basketball, stopping at the house to
look back, Tessy's head bowed over a knee poking up her
white dress.

∽

"I'm tired of this being small shit," Minkoff said.

I was shooting jumpers from the key and he'd appeared behind me.

"You'll grow," I said.

"Oh yeah?" he said. "When?"

"Hey," I said, "at least you're smart."

"Who gives a shit," he said, "if you can't dunk?"

"If you were tall you'd wish you were smart," I said.

"Nope," he said. "In this case, the grass is actually greener on the other side. It's a fact."

"Game to fifteen," I said. "Spot you eight."

Minkoff walked toward me, dragging his feet all hang-dog and mopey, then poked the ball from my arm and dribbled in for a lay-up.

"Nine nothing," he said with a grin.

At home I had missed dinner, so I grabbed an apple from the fridge and was walking out when my father walked in.

"I'm thinking of going out for basketball next year," I said.

"I'm sure you'll do fine," he said, filling a glass with water.

"You are?" I said.

He turned and smiled. "You need a little more belief in yourself."

"I believe in myself."

"Then you'll do fine," he said, and walked out.

I poked my head in Tessy's door, her room near dark, curtains closed. "Sleeping?" I asked.

"Thinking."

Her blanket was pulled up over her waist, revealing the top half of the white dress. I sat on the bed.

"You okay, Tess?"

"If everybody in the family goes away," she said, "Lonnie, Mom, Dad, in a way even you, Ricky."

As my eyes adjusted to the dark, I could see her dimly lit face.

"Why don't you come home for dinner?" Tessy said.

"I'd rather play basketball," I said.

I stood and opened the curtains, and Tessy gazed out at the dusky air.

"Everything's changing," she said.

"It'll be okay," I said.

"You're answering automatically," she said, gazing at me, her eyes barely visible in the dim light.

"Sometimes I get so scared," she said. "But I don't know of what."

"It'll be o–" I began but caught myself.

I remembered a storybook I'd read as a child about a little girl walking in the mountains who had met a shepherd that helped her find her way back. And though in the story the girl had gotten home safely, there was a dreamy, unreal quality to her return, and I remembered thinking she had actually died, that though on one level she had lived, something much darker had actually happened. The girl reminded me of Tessy, who always seemed to be living and dying at the same time.

"Just get some sleep," I said, standing, pulling the curtains closed, pausing in the doorway. "Okay?"

Tessy blinked slowly and tried to smile.

When school let out in June I took a job washing dishes at The House of Dogs, an Amagansett bar known for its summer crowds. My shifts ended late and the next day I wouldn't get up till afternoon.

One day, I saw Tessy sitting among rows of newly sprouted plants in blue jean cut-offs and a bikini top, and walked on out.

"How about a swim?" I said.

Tessy looked up, smiled like I didn't mean it, and returned to her weeds.

"Come on," I said, "the ocean's getting warmer."

"It's not the temperature."

Tessy kept pulling weeds, so I turned to go.

"Don't just leave," she said.

I stopped but she didn't say anything, so I again started off.

"Ricky."

"*What?*"

Again, Tessy wouldn't answer, so this time when she called I continued on to the house, changed into my shorts and sneakers, and walked to the court.

I found Minkoff inside the chain-link fence, sitting on his ball.

"You missed it," he said. "Eleven jumpers in a row. From deep."

"Not counting the ones you missed," I said.

"In a *row*, smart ass. Hey, Lance Williams was looking for you."

"Yeah?"

"A bunch of guys were playing this morning and he asked where you were."

"What'd you tell him?"

"You were home jerking off."

"You mention the picture of your mother?"

"Yes," he said, "I explained your fantasy about mating into a superior gene pool. They're coming back tomorrow."

Minkoff stood up and dribbled toward the basket.

"How'd you get so short?" I said.

"You don't *get* short," he said.

"You may as well take credit for it," I said. "It's your one exceptional quality."

"How'd you get so dumb?" he said.

"*You don't get dumb*," I squeaked, Minkoff flipping me off.

"Okay, little fella," I said. "One-on-one, full court."

I gave him the ball first and he turned out to indeed be hot, grabbing a quick lead, shouting out the score after each basket. When he went up five baskets, I turned it up a notch, closing the gap, and as we ran the court, up and back, up and back, I forgot the score and began to wonder about playing with Lance and the others on the team, practicing on the polished hardwood floor, playing before crowds of fans in the bleachers.

"Next basket wins," Minkoff said, dribbling toward me.

At the top of the key, he pulled up and hoisted a shot from his shoulder—nothing but net. Minkoff threw both fists into the air and circled the court.

Falling back against the fence at my side, Minkoff slid down to a sit.

"Congratulations on achieving your dream," I said.

"Shit," Minkoff said, "I'd give both nuts to be as good as you. You can shoot, handle the ball, jump like a freak, but you don't give a shit. If I had your talent, I'd be busting some ass."

"Ever think you're just jerking yourself, wanting what you can't have?"

"That is your area of expertise," he said. He stood up and released a long shot from his shoulder.

"You know, you really are short," I said.

"Two minutes ago, I mopped the floor with you."

"A fluke," I said.

"Blow me."

"I felt sorry for you."

"Alright, Sir Doesn't-Give-a-Shit. Bring your ass out here for another whipping."

I strolled out and scooped up the ball, took two dribbles to the basket, and dunked two-handed.

"You see?" Minkoff said. "You're a freak."

Minkoff grabbed the ball, stuck it in my stomach, and crouched low, feet spread, hands dangling between knees. "Do it now, circus boy!"

The next morning, I headed up to the court early and shot jump-shots, moving around the perimeter in a half circle from one corner to the other, and back again.

Lance's blue Taurus pulled up and four guys emerged—
Lance, Ben, and two others from the team, Henclik the
center, and Higgins, the point guard who lived near Lance
in Freetown.

The four of them strolled sleepily through the gate and
onto the court, high-top sneakers untied. Lance introduced
me and they each offered a lazy hand slap.

"I know your father," I said to Ben.

"What's the old coot up to?" he said, tossing up a shot.

"Fishing, I guess."

"Sounds about right," he said.

The big guy, Henclik, pulled in Ben's miss and Higgins,
the smallest on the court, called for the ball.

Higgins received the pass and flicked a smooth shot
from his forehead, which dropped directly through the
basket.

"Just cause I'm always settin up y'all," he said.

Henclik caught the ball and passed it back to Higgins,
who shot another that fell through.

"I'm telling you," Higgins said.

"Shit," Ben said, "you ain't no shooter." He grabbed the
ball and walked to the corner holding it on his hip.

"Alright, fisherman," Higgins said, moving over in
front of Ben, rotating the bill of his hat to the back, "show
me what you got."

Blood coloring his face, Ben, 5' 10" with broad shoulders
and ropey muscles, dropped the ball to the asphalt, dribbling
with his left hand, holding off Higgins with his hip. After
four dribbles he scooped up the ball and shot a fade-away
that bounced off the back of the rim.

"We gonna play or just watch these two?" Henclik said.

"Let's go," Higgins said, "me and Lance. Brothers against white boys."

Lance looked at me. "Ricky, you mind taking next? We'll play to seven."

"Seven?" Ben said. "Let's go fifteen."

"Yeah, fifteen," Henclik said.

"Seven," Lance said. "Ricky was here."

Lance and Higgins won the game and I played next with Henclik. Though they had the speed, Henclik dominated inside and we beat them. A few games later Lance and I took on Henclik and Ben, everyone's shirts now soaked through with sweat.

With Ben feeding Henclik down low, they took the lead, then Lance intercepted a pass, in the same motion flipping the ball out to me at the key, where I hit a jumper. We took the ball out and I hit Lance cutting to the basket. As he went up toward the rim, he drew both Henclik and Ben into the air and dropped the ball over his shoulder for me to lay it in. Game.

Lance strolled over and we slapped hands. "Way to shoot," he said.

"With passes like that, it's easy," I said.

Higgins strolled back onto the court. "Looks like the brothers win another," he said.

"Shit," Henclik said, "Ricky ain't no brother."

"He ain't?" Higgins said, looking at me cockeyed. "Sure as hell plays like one."

After everyone else had piled in the car, Lance, standing at the open door, looked back. "You coming out for the team?" he said.

"I don't know," I said.

"What do you mean you don't know?"

"I'll be a senior," I said, thinking it might not be worth it to play just one year.

Lance shook his head and smiled. "You'd rather play out here by yourself," he said.

"Not really," I said.

He held his eyes on me. "Be here tomorrow?" he said.

"Maybe," I said.

Lance shook his head and broke into a smile. "Boy don't know if he's coming or going," he said, and lowered himself into the car.

Chapter 4

SATURDAY NIGHT, LABOR Day weekend, the stream of dishes being hauled through the battered swinging door from the dining room began to ebb as dinner ended and the bar took over. The cook, an Ecuadorian guy named Manuel, cleaned the grill as we drank our after-the-rush beer. I loaded a rack of what was now mostly glasses, slid it through, and stacked it on the floor. When I got six racks, I carried them out to the bar.

Back in the kitchen, Manuel handed me the phone from the wall.

"Ricky," Tessy said, "you've got to come home."

Manuel agreeing to finish up for me, I pedaled down Indian Wells Highway into a humid summer breeze. Our driveway was dark, with only faint light filtering through the maple tree from the streetlamp.

"There was something here," Tessy said as I entered her room.

"Tessy, you can't drag me home from work every time a floorboard creaks."

Pain spread across her face. "Ricky, there's something after me."

"Okay," I said, pulling in a breath, sitting in the desk chair.

"I was just lying here in the dark and I could feel it enter. The pressure of the room changed."

Tessy inhaled deeply as the leaves washed against the window.

"I wanted to scream," she said.

"Then you should have."

"And wake Dad?"

I turned off the desk lamp, hoping she'd go to sleep, and the light from the streetlamp slid in patches across the floor onto the bed.

"I feel something," Tessy said.

I slid my chair closer. "It's okay, Tess."

As she grabbed my arm, her fingers pressing into my flesh, a wave of light swept across the ceiling and we heard the hum of a motor. I went to the window, Tessy not moving, staring across the room at the opposite wall, and saw a car partly hidden by the privet at the end of the driveway. As I headed down the stairs, I heard the kitchen door creak open, suck closed.

A dark figure stood in the kitchen.

"Boo," Lonnie said.

She walked over and hugged me, and blood surged through my body with the feel of her strong arms.

"You're bigger," she said.

"Nah."

She pushed me back to arm's length. "Jesus," she said, "you're a monster."

"We kept your room empty," I said.

"I'm not staying," she said. "Where's Tessy?"

"Her room."

I followed Lonnie up the stairs, and we found Tessy standing beyond the bed in the far corner. When she saw Lonnie, she ran over and grabbed her, releasing a sob as they embraced.

I helped Lonnie carry her easel down from the attic to her car and, returning, we met my father, wearing a bathrobe and slippers, in the kitchen.

"What's going on?" he asked.

"Nothing," Lonnie said, walking past.

"Lonnie," he said.

She stopped and turned back, one hand on a hip.

"We just loaded her easel," I said.

"How long have you been back?" he asked her.

"Couple of hours," she said, "why?"

"Is everything okay? You got a job?"

"Yes and no." Lonnie turned and walked from the room, and we heard her footsteps on the stairs.

My father raised his eyebrows. "She's got to come in the middle of the night?" he said.

I shrugged and headed up to Tessy's room where Lonnie said Carter was waiting, stepped over and gave me a hug.

At Tessy's door, Lonnie turned back.

"It's no big deal, I promise," she said to Tessy and left.

Tessy told me Lonnie was only in town to make some money helping her boyfriend paint some rich guy's house, and that she asked Tessy to go with them afterward back to Florida.

"I don't know," Tessy said, turning to the dark window. "What am I going to do in Florida?"

"What are you going to do here?" I said.

Tessy glared at me. "My family is here," she said.

In October the maples lining the street seemed to absorb the orange light from the shortening days, swelling in reds and yellows buffeted by the wind. When Minkoff came along to the gym to watch me try-out, I told him he should try-out for JV.

"Nah," Minkoff said, "my game isn't sharp at the moment."

The third and last day of try-outs, Coach strolled over when my group came off the court.

"You've lost some time," he said, "but you can definitely help the team."

Coach waited a second, watching for a reaction. Not getting one, he gave me a light smack on the shoulder.

"Practice tomorrow at three," he said, and headed to his office.

I took a seat on an open section of bleachers beside Ben.

"I just wonder where he's going to fit you in," he said.

"Sitting on the bench would be okay," I said.

"Nah," Ben said, standing, "he ain't keeping you to sit on the bench."

I took a few foul shots and, as I was leaving for the locker room, saw Minkoff's head poking through the doorway.

"You made it?" he said.

"Yeah."

"Yes!" he said, pumping a fist beside his shoulder. "Gansett boys kicking ass!"

By the second week of preseason practices, I had settled in as the sixth man, first sub off the bench, and split my time during practice between the red and gray teams, red being the first team, with Lance, Ben, Henclik, Higgins, and another guy from Freetown, Jerome Battle.

When at the end of practice, we'd scrimmage five-on-five, I'd start out with the grays, matching up against Lance who, out on the full floor, was even smoother than on the playground—more loping and fluid, more deceptive.

"Ready, cuz?"

Leaning on his knees, Lance eyed me, waiting for Coach to toss the ball up between us. Though Henclik was four inches taller, Lance jumped center, and I jumped for the second team.

"Last chance to fake a cramp, pull the fire alarm," Lance said.

"No need," I said.

Lance flashed a grin, offered a high-five, and proceeded to win the tip and ignore the called play, taking the ball straight at me, stutter-stepping, beating me to the rim. But before he could score, I leaped from behind and pinned the ball against the glass, sweeping it down in the same motion and passing it off.

"Boy *erased* your ass!" Higgins called as we ran up the court.

"Damn," Lance said, looking at me with glinting eyes, "I might have to start *playing*."

∞

After showering, I went for my bike and found Lance on the sidewalk waiting for his ride. I messed up the combination the first time and tried again, twisting to catch the light from an approaching car.

"Stash it in the trunk," Lance said.

"I don't mind riding."

The car stopped and a dark figure emerged, walking briskly past us toward the door.

"Joany!" Lance called. The figure redirected itself toward us. "My sister," Lance said.

"She in school?" I said.

"Nah."

Joany wore a woolen hat, puffed out by thick braids, and when Lance introduced us, offered a gentle handshake.

The horn honked.

"Sure you don't want a ride?" Lance said.

"Thanks anyway," I said.

Though it would be a five-mile ride, Amagansett was out of their way, Freetown over toward Three Mile Harbor. As they drove off, I saw Joany glance back through the window and wondered if I'd said something stupid, then twisted my gear bag over my shoulders, backpack style, and rode through town and turned onto the back roads, taking Further Lane to Amagansett.

I found Tessy in bed reading.

"Lonnie and Carter are still here," she said, lowering her book. "Staying in the house they're painting in Sag Harbor.

I've been hitching there instead of school." Sag Harbor was nine or ten miles away, on the bay side.

"Tessy, your school's private. Dad's paying for it."

"And this is why." She smiled sheepishly. "Public school'd be harder to cut."

"Lonnie sticking around?" I asked.

"They're going back to Florida next week. I told her I'd go," she said softly. Then her eyes widened. "Why don't you come?" she said.

"I've got basketball."

"*Basketball?*"

"I'm sixth man."

Tessy ran her fingers through her hair, freeing small knots. "Ricky, it's like, I don't know, winter's coming and I'm not sure what to do. Would it bother you if I went?"

I hesitated, sensing a trick question. "Of course," I said, "but if I knew it was good for you . . ."

"So you don't care," she said.

"Of course I care," I said.

But Tessy didn't respond, just stared out the window.

In my room I found a note from Minkoff *glued* to my closet door which said he'd borrowed my ball because his "could no longer perform the feats being demanded of it," which I took to mean it'd gone flat.

I biked through the dark to the court, stopping just outside the range of floodlights, and watched Minkoff walk up and down the court dribbling the ball back and forth between his legs, managing five or six times before losing control, muttering, and starting again.

"Your legs are too short," I said, walking into the light.

"What's the matter, hotshot," Minkoff said, "no interviews tonight?"

"Told 'em I had to check out my home-boy with the little legs."

"Check *this* out," he said. He hoisted a shot from the top of the key that missed everything.

"Don't make me come out there and school your ass," I said.

"*School?*" he said. "You been hanging out with the brothers too much. Cause I'm about to *kick* your ass."

After a long game, in which we lost track of the score, we slumped against the fence and waited for the lights, set with a timer, to shut off at ten.

"So how is it?" Minkoff said.

"Okay."

"Those guys as good as everyone says?"

"I guess."

Minkoff removed his glasses and adjusted the elastic band.

"Jesus," he said, glancing up at the spotlights nailed to a tree at the far corner, "it's gotta be ten. If the lights don't go off, let's play another."

"They'll go off."

Minkoff stood up and dribbled toward the hoop, lights clicking off as he pulled up to shoot, his voice slicing through the dark.

"*Minkoff shoots out the lights—literally shoots out the lights!*" Then a roar from the crowd—Minkoff releasing air from deep in his throat.

"Come on, Dream-time," I said, "let's cruise."

The ball bounced slowly toward me through the dark, and I grabbed my bike and we walked down Minkoff's street, dark stretches between the streetlights, and on to Minkoff's house in the middle of a dark stretch, the house dark too.

"Where's your mom?" I asked.

"Got some boyfriend, manfriend, I don't know. She's been getting all dressed up, asking me how she fucking smells."

He walked up onto the porch, then spun back. "Listen, Ricky," he said, "I want you to kick some ass this season."

"I'll try, buddy."

He raised a fist. "Be cool, bro."

"See you, Minkoff."

He walked into the house, and I waited for a light to go on, but none did, and walking home glanced back, the house still dark except for one window on the second floor in the back, Minkoff's bedroom, dimly illuminated by the light from his television.

Tessy's door open a crack but the light off, I continued past, stripped to my boxers, and climbed in bed. Out my window, I could see small points of light through the limbs of the tree that had lost most of its leaves. Gazing at a group of low bright stars, I remembered how Tessy, Lonnie, and I used to go to the beach with Mom and Dad, lie on blankets and watch for shooting stars, how every few minutes Mom and Dad would gasp and point, but how we three children never seemed to see them.

Chapter 5

AFTER PRACTICE I WAS bikeless, having taken the bus to school because of a cold morning rain, so I headed out with Lance to where his mom was waiting and slid into the back seat. He introduced his mother as Jackie, and when she turned to shake my hand, saying she knew Lonnie, I recognized her from the rug store in East Hampton where Lonnie used to work.

"She's something, that Lonnie," Jackie said. "Still painting?"

"Far as I know."

Jackie invited me to dinner and when I said no thanks, Lance said to his mother, "Boy don't know how to say yes. Course he's eating with us."

Their house, a renovated barn with cedar shingles and black trim, sat only a few feet off the road, just after the trailer park that marked the beginning of Freetown.

Lance and I sat on stools at the kitchen counter opposite Jackie who chopped vegetables and tossed them into a sizzling pan. Joany entered and walked straight past us to the refrigerator, dragging stockinged feet, her hair now in an afro flattened on one side.

"Good morning, Joan," Lance said.

She flashed a brief smile, poured herself a glass of juice, and walked off, pausing at the doorway to say "Hi Ricky" without looking back, and continuing on.

"How's it going?" I called after her.

"Very slowly," she answered from the next room.

"Don't mind her," Lance said. "She's in a state of permanent heart-break."

"She'll come out of it," Jackie said.

"When she's a wrinkled old bat," he said.

"How soon they forget." Jackie turned to me. "You should have seen Mr. Man here a month ago."

"I didn't go into hibernation," Lance said.

"Hardly ate for two weeks," Jackie said. "Lost fifteen pounds."

"I was dieting."

"Darn near flunked out of school—on the phone every night to Pennsylvania."

Lance's voice climbed into a falsetto. *She came back, didn't she?*

Jackie served minute steaks, mashed potatoes, and a mix of fried vegetables, then went into the next room.

Two bites into my meal, Lance's little brother, Trip, head barely reaching the doorknob, burst through the kitchen door as if propelled by the cold air behind him and flopped back against the door.

Lance introduced us, and I extended a hand.

"Lance said you're the best white guy on the team," Trip said, shaking my hand.

I looked at Lance.

"Once you get used to Coach's system," he said, "you'll be starting, no question. Move Ben to the bench."

Lance turned back to Trip, asked about each of his classes, rubbed his head, and told him to go wash up for dinner. Then he slumped on an elbow and poked at his food.

"First time you been out here?" he said. "To Freetown?"

"First time to somebody's house."

Lance kept poking at his food.

"It's nice," I said. "Your mom seems cool."

"She is," Lance said, still looking down. "She is cool."

After we cleaned up, Trip took me upstairs to see his collection of sketches.

Lance called up that he'd take me home now or I could sleep on the futon. Halfway down the stairs, I saw Joany lying on the futon watching TV.

"I'll take the futon," I said.

Joany jerked her head around and glared at me.

"Kidding," I said, and she turned back to the set.

As I followed Lance to the door, I heard Joany's voice. "Goodbye," she called.

"Goodbye," I called back.

At home, I walked into Tessy's room where she and Lonnie were talking and sat on the bed.

"If you don't find a job," Lonnie said to Tessy, "you come back home."

"For you it's nothing," Tessy said, "you just get up and go. It's not so easy for me."

Lonnie put an arm across Tessy's shoulders. "It'll be fine."

"What happens if I can't do it?" Tessy said. "What happens if I'm down there and I can't get a job, can't pay rent?"

"The hardest part is the first step," Lonnie said. "After that it gets easy."

"You're going?" I asked Tessy.

A nervous smile worked its way through her gloom. "Looks like it," she said. "What do they grow down there?" she said to Lonnie.

"Oranges," Lonnie said.

"What can I grow?" Tessy said.

"Anything you want," Lonnie said.

"Lettuce?"

"Best place in the world for lettuce," Lonnie said.

"I won't go if I can't have a garden."

"You *can*," Lonnie said.

"What about Ricky?" Tessy said.

"I'll be fine," I said. "With basketball, I'm hardly even here."

"Jackie tells me you're playing on the same team as Lance," Lonnie said.

"Are you sure?" Tessy said to me.

"Positive."

"Okay then," Lonnie said, "Carter wants to drive straight through, so be ready at six sharp." She walked over to me. "I'll see you at Christmas." She hugged me, then pushed me back to arm's length. "Score some baskets for your sisters," she said.

Lonnie walked out, and Tessy slid a suitcase out from under the bed.

"What's going to happen with school?" I asked.

"I can go down there."

"Seriously? You think once you get there, you're going to sign up for school?"

"And what exactly would I be missing?"

"You can't go to college if you don't go to high school."

"If that's your plan, go ahead," Tessy said, "Mr. Chip off the Block."

"Tessy, you've got to be doing something."

She hesitated, then said, "You know what Mom told me when she found out she had cancer, when she realized it was advanced?"

"What?" I said.

"'It's better this way.'" Tessy lifted a stack of clothes from her dresser and carried them to the open suitcase. "I came home from school, and she asked me to sit with her on the patio. 'I'm going to tell you something,' she said, but first, she made me promise to remember that no matter what she was about to say, I needed to understand that everything was going to be for the better. So I said okay, and she said, 'I have cancer.'

"Then she goes and dies, and I kept telling myself, 'It's for the better. Somehow, it's for the better.'"

Tessy shook her head and stared at me. "Better for her," she said. "That's what she meant. Better for her."

The next morning, Saturday, I found Tessy's room empty and felt a swirl of mixed feelings. I was afraid she'd have a hard time but also hopeful at the prospect of change, and maybe a little relieved.

I headed toward the beach, the temperature down in the forties, and found the Brister crew a few hundred yards east backing the dory down to the surf, today wind-chopped from a southwesterly breeze.

Wesley's oldest son, Jason, and the fourth hand, whose name was Duff, climbed in and Wesley and the other son, Petey, slid the boat into the water, shoving it into the breakers. Jason lowered the outboard motor, and they sliced through the waves and headed out to sea, Duff dumping armfuls of net over the side as Jason steered the boat through a gradual arc.

"Hop in, boy," Wesley said, Petey entering the other truck.

I climbed in the cab, and we drove slowly up the beach to meet the dory. His face ruddy from the cold, Wesley leaned forward over the wheel gazing intently ahead, and I wondered if he had to work harder because he didn't have Ben.

"The Indians out here used to say each man gets one season of fish," he said, peering forward. "A stage of life, maybe eight, ten years. Hell, if us Brister men done used up ours—" he shot me a glance— "maybe you got one coming."

"If I do, it's all yours," I said.

Wesley stopped the truck and backed the trailer to the edge of the water. Before getting out, he winked at me. "Done cashed in our hope," he said, "but still got us a prayer."

Jason and Duff glided in on a small wave nearly to the beach and threw a rope to Wesley, who affixed it to the winch in the back of the truck and switched on the motor. The steel paten wound in the rope, raising the dory onto the trailer, and Wesley affixed the net to the winch and began winding in the quarter mile or so of seine, Petey driving slowly toward us with the other end.

All were quiet as they waited, Wesley watching the winding winch for knots in the net. As Petey pulled up beside us, the net almost in, Jason and Duff waded into the surf to help pull with their hands and for a moment the catch looked good, the trapped fish boiling out of the water. But once they'd pulled the last of the net onto shore, the mood slumped, the men silently sorting the fish into burlap sacks—bass, porgies, sea robins, a few mackerel— the largest sack containing sea robins, too boney to eat, which Jason dragged to the surf and emptied.

Their black Labrador, Guts, trotted to each man, nervously wagging his tail against the silence.

Once the net had been gathered, the meager catch stashed, I climbed in Wesley's truck, Jason following, wedging me in the middle.

At the parking lot, Wesley sold the dozen or so blue fish to a group of weekenders, giving the last one free to a guy who only had a fifty, and stood there answering questions about how best to prepare them. Jason grabbed a beer from a cooler behind the seat, popped it open, and slumped down, the bill of his cap over his face.

I slid out the driver's side and said goodbye to Wes, who turned from a customer and smiled through deep creases.

"You take her easy," he said.

◦◦◦

No practice until afternoon, I wandered through the house to the sunroom on the far side where Dad and Gladys sat reading newspapers over coffee.

"Tessy and Lonnie left," I said.

Gladys looked up. "I thought Lonnie was in Florida."

"She came back," my father said.

"When?" Gladys said. "Why didn't I know?" I shrugged and she looked at my father. "Harold, how long was she back?"

"Couple of weeks," he said, still reading his paper.

"They left," I said.

Gladys sighed. "I didn't know she was back." She looked at me. "Tessy left us a note saying she was moving in with friends."

"She didn't mention Lonnie?" I said.

My father shook his head.

"Harold," Gladys said.

"What do you want me to do?" he said.

"You should have told me Lonnie was back."

"Lonnie's back," he said.

Gladys' eyes flared and she shook her head, looking at me. "Oh," she huffed, "this father of yours."

"Well," I said, "they left."

Chapter 6

As October turned to November on the East End, the sun carved a lower arc across the sky and the light dimmed to burnt orange. The sky filled out with a steady cover of clouds, and the fishermen, when they weren't on the bay side eeling, spent long hours in their trucks, parked at the end of the road, keeping vigils before the sea.

Preparing for the first game, we practiced each day after school and on Saturday mornings. The second Saturday, I sat on the side as the first team ran through a new play that led to a jump shot from the corner for either Ben on one side or Lance on the other. Lance made most of his, but Ben was ice cold, Coach looking on in silence, only breaking it to utter the command, "Again."

When Ben's shot barely hit the rim, Higgins, passing Ben on his way back to his spot at the point, said, "Bro, you got to make that shot."

"Don't worry about it," Ben said.

"I'm worrying," Higgins said, stopping.

Lance passed between them, pushing Higgins back toward the point, and they again ran the play to Ben's side.

This time when he missed, Coach called my name, and Ben and I switched places.

We ran the play four times to my side and after missing the first, I made three straight.

"That's what I'm talking about," Higgins said, throwing me a high-five.

We switched back to Lance's side, and he ended the practice with a high-arcing fall-away from deep in the corner that dropped straight through. Higgins and I slapped palms, but Lance just turned and walked off.

I sat beside Lance on the wood bench before our lockers, pulled off my sneakers, peeled away my socks.

"He's definitely working you in," Lance said. "Couple more weeks, you'll be our top player."

"Right," I said.

"If you want it," he said.

"What are you talking about?" I said.

Lance stood up wrapped at the waist in a towel. "It's right there for you, man. Go ahead and take it." He gave me a wistful smile and walked off to the showers.

Dressed, Lance slung his backpack over a shoulder and turned to me. "Let's go eat," he said.

We walked out front and stood beside the building waiting for his mother, clouds of our smoky breath rising and dispersing in the cold air.

Two cheerleaders, one of them Ben's girlfriend, Donna, came out the door and walked by, stopping a little way off where she called over to me. As I approached, Donna stepped away from her friend and looked out across the dusky field.

"It's Ben," she said. "I broke up with him last week, but he keeps calling, last night at two-thirty." She turned to me and, barely visible in the near dark, her eyes were hard, angry. "What the hell is wrong with him?"

"I hardly talk to him," I said.

"Some people are so—" her face went sour— "so *thick*."

"Yeah, well . . ."

"What's going on with you?" she said. "You been hanging out with Lance?"

"A little."

"I heard you go to his house."

"*What?*"

"Forget it," she said, and she reached over and touched my arm as her ride pulled up. "Maybe say something to Ben," she said, and jogged off toward the waiting car.

"What'd she want?" Lance asked when I rejoined him beside the school.

"Trying to break up with Ben."

Lance bounced up and down, peering down the street. "This mean you're taking over?"

"No way."

"Good," he said, still looking down the street. "Nothing against Donna, but her brother isn't good for this town."

"He's a cop, right?"

"One who gets a special kick out of working Freetown."

"Stupidity must be a family trait," I said.

"Tell 'em, Rick." Lance smiled, still bouncing on his toes, then started weaving and bobbing, flicking jabs at me.

He began to circle, and we sparred open-handed, exchanging a series of short smacks. Then I landed one a little hard and Lance retaliated with a palm to my cheekbone, and I was coming back at him with a flurry when we heard a honk. Lance threw up his hands, and we high-fived and walked to the car.

In the Williams' living room, a cylinder lamp on the floor threw a cone of light up the wall that opened into a circle on the ceiling, beneath which Joany lay on her stomach on the futon writing, her back sloping down and arcing up to her butt. Lance went upstairs to make a call, and I sat in the easy chair watching Joany, the end of the pen in her mouth, staring at the wall.

"Letter?" I asked.

Ignoring me, Joany blinked slowly and pushed her tongue under her lip like she was searching for something profound, her short afro shaped into a smooth orb, each earlobe flecked with a tiny gold stud.

"Tell 'em Lance made preseason All-Long Island," I said.

She looked at me completely expressionless, then turned back to the far wall.

"Tell 'em I flunked my French test."

Joany feigned writing with exaggerated strokes, and read aloud, "Ricky Hawkins flunked his French test," and looked at me. "Can I write my letter now?"

"If you can think of something to say."

I shuffled through some magazines, then turned on the television, Joany releasing a loud sigh, then when I asked if she minded, saying no.

"You ought to be in the movies," I said.

"What makes you think I'm not?"

"Maybe a silent movie."

"I'm writing to an art school in Boston," she said.

"You paint?"

"I sculpt." She eyed me a moment then dropped the pad on the futon and walked up the stairs, returning with a bust of a woman with sharp features and a thick mane of hair slung back, eyes angled like a panther's, deep holes in the clay for pupils.

"It's a self-portrait," she said.

"That's *you?*"

"It's an impression. An interpretation."

We heard loud footsteps and Trip stomped into the room, announced that Lance was upstairs on the phone, and continued on to the kitchen where Jackie was cooking.

"Girlfriend," Joany said.

"Who is she?" I said.

She huffed and shook her head. "Do you two even *talk* to each other?"

"So how come you quit school?" I asked.

"Art department."

"But if you quit, how can you go to college?"

"It's an *institute*. The whole world doesn't revolve around high school diplomas."

Joany resumed her letter and Jackie called me and Lance, who shuffled down the stairs, and the two of us sat at the kitchen counter, the windows steamed, air thick with the smell of herbs and tomato sauce.

Jackie's hairline was set back on her forehead and she had dark brown eyes with crow's feet, each one an intricate network of lines.

"So what do you hear from those globetrotting sisters of yours?" Jackie asked, dishing out spaghetti with copper tongs, ladling on sauce.

"I got a letter from Tessy that said she's sleeping on the couch. Carter and Lonnie are both bartenders and there's only two rooms."

"Lonnie will figure something out," Jackie said, Lance and I beginning to eat. "She's a fighter. I saw that as soon as she started working for me.

"Must have been her second or third day in the shop," Jackie said. "A customer was giving me a hard time. City guy, dressed in a blazer, loafers, you know the type. Asked me how this one rug could be hand-woven with such a regular pattern, and I was, well, the truth is, I didn't know much about rugs in the beginning, just had a connection to a wholesale distributor and figured what the hell. So I made something up about a particular style from Turkey, and the guy said, "You should stick to rugs from your own country" and turned to leave.

"Before he reached the door, Lonnie cut him off. 'Because you live on Park Avenue and wear a linen blazer on a Saturday afternoon,' she said, 'you know where everybody comes from?' She was fourteen years old, and I'm telling you, she had that man *on his heels.*"

"Tessy's the one that might have trouble down there," I said.

"Then she can come back," Jackie said. "Sometimes going away helps you realize how much there is right here."

"This ain't exactly Motor City," Lance said.

Jackie stared at him, spoon in one hand, potholder in the other. "If you see dull, it's because you are dull."

"I know, I know." Lance turned to me. "You see a car accident, she'll blame you, say you were looking for trouble."

"Lance, it just gets old, you moping about how boring it is out here. You got a warm home, you got family . . . "

"Okay, okay," Lance said, turning to me. "Coach fixing to start you against Longwood," he said.

I kept looking at Jackie, expecting her to continue, but she only shook her head and set down the potholder and spoon.

"Who says?" I said to Lance.

"He's working you in, working Ben out, plain as day."

"Yeah, well . . . " I said.

"Yeah well nothing," Lance said. "You want to play and you know it."

After dinner, we took the Taurus to the deli in Bridgehampton where Lance didn't get ID'd for beer, then headed to Georgica Beach. We pulled into the empty lot and shined the lights toward the breakers, but the lights made a haze, so Lance flicked them off and as our eyes adjusted, we saw rows of white rolling in from the blackness. We each took a beer and Lance rolled down his window, leaned back in the breeze, and I sat there sipping, watching the ocean split into a white line and go black, and split into a white line.

After a while Lance tilted his head toward me and started the car. "Time for you to meet my girl," he said.

At the traffic-light in town we pulled up beside a police car.

"Beer down," Lance said. "Got Donna's brother on night patrol."

Leaning back on the head rest, the cop swiveled his head and took a good look at us before the light changed.

"I think that's the guy pulled Lonnie over and asked her on a date," I said.

"She go?"

"Told him she'd take the ticket."

We headed through town, through Freetown, and on to Springs, entering a stretch of woods, then a clearing for a horse farm opening out beneath the dark sky, and pulled in a driveway before a dark strip of harbor. Lance led up a flight of outdoor stairs and knocked, a blonde woman, too old I figured to be Lance's girl, answering in a terry cloth robe cinched around her waist.

"This is Ricky," Lance said. Then to me, "Tanya."

She let us in, and we sat on the couch, Tanya turning off the TV and bringing us each a beer.

"Where you been?" Tanya said.

"Nowhere special," Lance said.

Tanya turned to me. "Where do you live, Ricky?"

"Amagansett."

"No wonder you're hanging out with this guy," she said. "Amagansett's a ghost town in the winter."

"That's why he lives there," Lance said. "He's a ghost."

Tanya looked at Lance. "My father's back in the hospital," she said.

"I can't go," Lance said.

"I'm not asking," she said, and stood up and walked to the window. Lance walked over and slid his arms around her waist.

"My mother's flipping about my grades," he said. "Let me drop Ricky and I'll come back." Lance walked to the door. "You want me to?" he said, turning.

Tanya glanced from Lance to me, smiling playfully. "Eh," she said, "depends what's on TV."

The Taurus heater whirred against the evening cold as we drove along the empty road through the woods toward Amagansett.

"Her old man's got cancer," Lance said. "She's been going back and forth to Pennsylvania. She's twenty-three."

Lance pulled into my driveway, and we sat for a minute looking up at the dark house, silhouetted beneath the star-lit sky.

"Looks like that house in *Psycho*," he said.

"Sometimes it feels like it," I said.

"Who all's in there, anyway? You never told me."

"Just my father and step-mother."

"Step-mother a witch or what?"

"Kind of took over the place."

"Whenever you want, you can stay at my house," Lance said, his face flickering in the light from the streetlamp above the leaves.

"All my shit's here," I said.

"Just know you got that option," he said, and we slapped palms.

A sheet of plastic blocked the front stairs—my father's attempt to cut down on heating oil—so I used the back flight and saw a crack of light under Dad and Gladys' door. I continued down the hall to my room, flopped down on the bed and wondered about Lance and Tanya, how exactly their relationship worked. If high school kids were all romance and drama, and adults all business, they seemed somewhere in between.

Unable to lie still, I climbed out onto the roof of the front porch which wrapped around the corner of the house and ended at the edge of Dad and Gladys' lit-up window. I walked over and leaned onto the ledge beneath it. Through a gap beneath the curtains, I saw Gladys standing in the middle of the room in a white nightgown, eying herself in the full-length mirror. A table lamp behind her revealed the silhouette of her body through the nightgown. She placed some pins in her hair, gave herself a contented nod, and walked into the adjoining bathroom.

My father, sitting on the bed, reached slowly down to remove each of his shoes, then each sock, his back more arched, shoulders more slumped, than I remembered. He placed his hands on his thighs and hoisted himself up, straightening, not quite all the way, unbuttoning the shirt, easing it off, his stomach and chest wide but his limbs gaunt, slowly losing their muscle. Down to his boxers, he settled himself back on the bed.

Gladys slid under the covers on the opposite side, said something, and my father again hoisted himself to a stand and walked into the bathroom, returning with a glass of water and handing it to her. She set it on the table and turned off the light.

Back at my window, I sat on the sill, gazing out at the dark figures of trees, the last of November's leaves rustling in the breeze, dead on the limbs. The sky above was black, with low clouds wisping past. I breathed the cold air deep into my lungs and listened to the wind in the leaves.

Chapter 7

I N THE LOCKER room after the Longwood game, Henclik, who'd committed five turnovers, sat on the bench shaking his head and Coach came by and told him not to bring the ball up the court but get it to a guard.

"And you," he said to me, "I need you to dial in."

I had committed my own share of turnovers and played the wrong defense three times in a row, Coach yelling at me from the bench.

"Anyway," Coach said, turning to the others, "wasn't just these two who messed up. Takes an entire team to play that bad."

Coach exited and Higgins stepped up. "Like in the first half, Battle falling down—" Higgins threw out his arms, stumbling— "in the open floor, nobody near him."

"Too much paint on the mid-court line," Battle said.

"You should run like Henclik," Lance said, stepping over, pantomiming Henclik's stiff, high-stepping strides.

"Henclik, man," Higgins said, "how come you don't make a monster movie?"

"Fuck you, Higgins," Henclik said, still looking down.

"I'm serious, man. Them big Godzilla steps . . ."

"How about Ricky out there playing zone all by himself," Lance said, "and his man standing under the basket butt naked?"

"I thought Coach gonna explode," Higgins said. "Battle's mother behind the bench muttering and shit, wrapped her scarf around her head, *still* heard Coach cussing." The pitch of Higgins' voice rose, his head bobbing. "'I ain't drove all the way up-island listen to no white man speaking 'bout putting his foot in somebody's you-know-what!'"

"What about Lance out there tippy-toing?" I said.

They all went quiet.

"Say what?" Battle said.

"When he got his fourth foul, he didn't go *near* the boards. Stood outside calling for the ball."

"I heard that." Higgins waved his hands. "'Give it up, I'm open, I'm open.' Motherfucker open alright."

"Standing at mid-court," Battle said, "calling 'I'm open.'"

"Standing out in the parking lot," Higgins said. "Give it up! Nobody near me!"

Now, even Henclik's gloom had lifted, and we all trooped into the shower, Higgins and Battle still ragging Lance.

Jackie left the Taurus at the school and six of us piled in and went for beer in Bridgehampton. I sat in the front between Lance and Higgins—Henclik, Battle, and Ben in the back. We cruised Main Street, then hit the beaches, finding a car full of girls at Georgica. It looked like Ben's ex, Donna, on the far side in the back, but it was too dark to be sure. Higgins rolled down the window and motioned their window down, Henclik and Battle slap fighting in the back, Ben beside them silently drinking.

"Don't mind these kids," Higgins called over. "Me and Ricky here—y'all know Ricky, right?—we were just saying how annoying it is hanging out with young boys."

"Is that Lance driving?" the girl at the passenger's window said.

"Yeah," Higgins said. "Like I was saying, me and *Lance* were just discussing—"

"Lance, you been over to Tanya Carlton's tonight?" the girl called.

"We had a game," Higgins said.

The girl took a sip from a plastic jug. "Where's Tanya?" she said.

"Roll it up, Kyle," Lance said to Higgins.

Higgins held him off with a hand. "Where you girls headed tonight?"

"Who wants to know?"

"Shit," Higgins said, "we got three white boys in here."

"Yeah, a Polack, a fisherman, and . . ." the girl broke off, turning back into the car, girl in the far corner leaning forward into the light—Donna.

"And a deaf mute," the girl added, apparently referring to me.

"You hear this shit?" Higgins said to me. "Say something."

"Like what?" I said.

"Anything."

"Bunch of bitches," Battle said from the back.

Ben leaned forward. "Who are they?" he said.

"Nobody," I answered.

Ben kept peering over at the car but Donna was back in the shadow. "Bitches," he grumbled, and slumped back in his seat.

Lance continued peering ahead at the ocean. "Roll it up, Kyle," he said to Higgins.

"Hey," Higgins called over. "What kind of prizes they give you—trophies, ribbons? Cause y'all definitely some world-class bitches."

"You want to see our prizes?" the girl at the window called back.

"You talk a lot of shit for somebody never even *seen* a dick," Higgins said.

The driver leaned over, calling, "So let's see one."

"Go home and ask your Daddy," Higgins said, and rolled up the window.

Lance backed up, the girls honked, and Higgins asked him to stop so he could whip out his dick and Lance said if he got out he wasn't getting back in, and we drove to Bridgehampton for more beer.

"Damn, Ricky," Higgins said, "them bitches liked *Battle* much as you. Lance, why we carrying these white boys?"

Lance didn't answer.

"Cause they sure ain't bringing in no women," Higgins grumbled.

When we got pulled over by Donna's brother, everyone was asleep except for Lance and me.

"What's going on, officer?" Lance said.

"Where you fellas headed?"

"Why?"

"I'm asking you, where you headed."

"I'm asking why."

"You been drinking?"

"Did I do something wrong?"

"Routine check."

"My ass," Lance muttered.

"What's that?" The cop leaned in the window.

"How's it going, Danny?" It was Ben, woken up.

"Ben?"

"We had a late game up at Longwood," Ben said.

The cop looked at Lance. "Guess you just never learned your manners."

I tapped Lance on the shoulder, trying to calm him, and he rolled up his window and we drove off.

"Fucking Danny," Ben said, slumping down low in the seat, eyes nearly closed.

"You think that red-neck is funny?" Higgins said, everybody now awake. "That's the third time he's pulled one of us over this week."

"He just doesn't take shit," Ben said, gazing drunkenly ahead.

"What the fuck are you talking about?" Higgins said.

"You don't like him," Ben said, "cause he won't take your shit."

"Stop the car, Lance," Higgins said, but Lance kept driving. "I'm not foolin', Williams," Higgins said, "stop the fucking car!"

Lance pulled over and Higgins jumped out. "I ain't *listening* to this bullshit," he said, and slammed the door.

We watched Higgins walk up the embankment to the sidewalk, drove along the shoulder beside him for a while, but Higgins wouldn't look at us, and Lance accelerated out onto the street, leaving him behind.

First, we dropped Henclik at the edge of the village, then took Ben to the school where he'd left his truck.

"You sure you want to drive?" Lance said out the window.

"What," Ben said, "I'm safer with you driving?"

"Just checking," Lance said, and we watched Ben fumble for his keys and climb in his truck.

The last three of us drove in silence out to Freetown, Lance pulling over at the end of a long dirt drive that disappeared into the woods, Battle getting out, Lance lowering his window.

"I got a blanket in the back if you want to borrow it," Lance said. "Awful cold out in them woods."

"Jackie'll keep me warm," Battle said, and he reached in Lance's window to smack each of our palms, then walked off down the driveway.

Down to the two of us, we pulled in Lance's driveway and sat in the car.

"You believe that cop?" Lance said.

"Trying to break the boredom," I said.

"It ain't boredom, Ricky."

"Then it's stupidity." I opened the door.

"Don't say that, man."

I closed the door and sat still.

"If that's how you feel, okay," Lance said, "but don't come over my house and tell me the motherfucker is pulling me over, telling me mind my manners because he's bored."

I didn't answer but stared straight ahead as our breath fogged the windshield.

"I knew this was going to happen," Lance said.

"What?"

"We'd be tight up to a point, then you'd hop out shaking your head, saying 'whatever.'"

"Nobody's hopping out."

"But you're thinking about it."

"You don't know what I'm thinking."

"Then what's this 'breaking the boredom' shit?"

"I was hoping it would just pass by, Lance."

"Well, it ain't."

"Then maybe you're right. Maybe I don't understand."

"Because you don't want to."

"Because I don't want to sit out here in the cold bitching about some cop with nothing better to do than fuck with a bunch of high school kids."

"He wasn't fucking with you, Ricky."

"The only one who had a pass was Ben."

He turned and looked out his window. "That's bullshit," he said.

"This is going nowhere." I got out of the car and Lance jumped out his side, came around and cut me off.

"Where you want it to go?" he said.

"Forget it." I turned away but he grabbed my shoulder and spun me back. I held up both hands, palms facing him. "Just let me leave. I'll walk home."

"'Cause it ain't going nowhere?"

"Cause everybody's your fucking enemy. Everybody's out to get Lance Williams."

"As long as you're living in a different world, thinking you're being fucked with same as us, maybe everybody is."

We glared at each other another moment, then Lance shook his head and turned away.

This time I cut him off. "Say whatever you want, say I got it made in the shade"—I pointed at my head—"but don't tell me what I'm thinking."

Lance waited a moment, then shook his head and walked inside. I paced the driveway, my skin burning, and opened my jacket to the cold. I started walking off down the street but after a couple hundred yards turned back.

I found Lance leaning against the car, gazing up at the sky, and took a spot beside him.

"I get there's shit I don't understand," I said. "But Lance, I come out here to Freetown, see you and your family, and it just doesn't look so bad."

"Oh no?"

"You don't see me inviting you to my house."

"No," he said, "I don't. But Ricky," and he paused, waiting till I looked him in the eye, "don't be so sure."

"About what?" I said.

"About how things look."

Chapter 8

A s WINTER SETTLED in on the island, windy and cold, I spent as little time as possible at home, which was being used more and more for Sentinels meetings, the gatherings mostly comprised of weekenders, second-home owners from New York.

One night after practice I came in after a meeting, last guy to leave saying goodbye in the kitchen dressed in tennis whites, probably on his way to one of the East Hampton estates with a tennis bubble.

Once the door had sucked closed, Gladys hustled over to the oven to remove a pan of chicken.

"Hungry?" she asked me.

"Yeah," I said, grabbing dishes and setting the table for three.

We sat down before the chicken—couple legs, couple breasts—and a bowl of steamed carrots. I took a bite of the chicken and began to chew, the chicken tough, leathery, no doubt cooked during the meeting.

"I hope it's not too dry," Gladys said.

"How long did it cook?" I said.

"Just what the cookbook said," Gladys answered. "Thirty minutes a pound."

"You used a cookbook?"

"I like to be sure," she said.

"What dish is this?" I asked.

"Roast herb chicken."

My mother used to roast chickens all the time, only she roasted whole ones, not cut-ups.

"Maybe the thirty minutes a pound meant for a whole chicken," I said.

"This *is* a whole chicken," Gladys said.

"An *intact* chicken," I said.

"Since when are you an expert on cooking?" my father said.

"I'm not. I know absolutely nothing. But Mom used to—"

"I'm sure your mother was a terrific cook," Gladys said.

My father held his eyes on me, looking baffled. "You mean that chicken and rice thing she used to make?"

"Yeah," I said, "with all the juices mixed in."

"She would cook the rice right in with the chicken," he said, still gazing at me.

"There are many ways to cook chicken," Gladys said.

"Nothing but rice, garlic, a little salt and pepper," my father said.

"She must have used herbs," Gladys said. "Thyme, maybe rosemary."

My father sat there looking at me. "She'd be chatting away," he said, "and she'd pop the skin off a couple garlic cloves, sprinkle on a little salt, little pepper, and slide it in the oven. Couple hours later, bingo."

"Harold," Gladys said, "the herbs are what give it the flavor."

My father turned and looked at her.

"She must have used something more than salt and pepper," Gladys said.

My father gazed at her another moment, then straightened in his chair. "Probably rosemary," he said. "And now that I think of it, maybe a little thyme."

The two of them eyed each other a moment. Then Gladys nodded and returned her attention to her food.

Most nights after practice, I went to Lance's. Sometimes Lance would stick around to do homework—not me, I had a first-period study hall where I'd scramble to do what I could—though usually he went off to Tanya's, leaving me behind to watch television with Joany.

One night over Christmas break I biked over in the early dark after practice, Lance already at Tanya's, and saw the familiar silvery glow in the windows. No longer knocking, I found Joany in the living room perched on the edge of the easy chair, knees splayed apart, mug clasped in both hands, peering at the TV. She must have known it was me because she didn't turn when I entered the room.

"Okay," she said at the commercial, "this journalist chick's boyfriend is meeting some men to do a business deal but the men are in the mob, so she's following him. Once again, the woman will have to save the man."

The movie, black and white, from the 50s or 60s, came back on and Joany tilted her head forward, watching from the tops of her eyes as a woman in a black dress and hat scurried into Yankee Stadium, bought a ticket, saw the guy in a box seat and snagged a seat a couple of rows back.

"Right," I said, "just grab a box seat."

"It's a *movie*," Joany said. "Watch the cinematography."

The next camera shot was from ground level of a vendor towering above, followed by a close-up of two men, one man's fleshy face raucously cheering, beside him the other face concealed in shadow.

Joany turned to me. "You see?"

"Something bad's going to happen," I said.

Then the boyfriend walked out to the concession area, the girl following but losing sight.

"Why, Marge," the guy said, startling her, grabbing her arm from the side. "What brings you out to the park?"

"Uh," she stammered, "I'm, I'm covering the game for Louie. He's home sick."

"Doesn't look good for the home team," the guy said.

"No, Billy," she said, "looks like you're, I mean *they're* in over their heads."

"Give me a break," I groaned.

Joany turned back to me. "It's true," she said, "the man goes out and gets in trouble, and the woman has to clean up the mess."

"Why doesn't she tell him what's happening?" I asked.

"Can't blow her cover."

Joany then predicted the final scene, in which the moment Billy realizes his predicament Marge has the police ready to go, and after a shoot-out, Billy, feeling proud but a little suspicious at how everything worked out, meets up with Marge back at the newspaper.

As the two of them exit the building and stroll off down the street, I watch closely as the camera pulls away and pans along a stone wall, on which is a series of dark distorted shapes, the jagged shadows of buildings we can't see.

"How'd you know the end?" I asked.

"The good guy—good girl," she said, "only triumphs once they've given up something."

"Was that a triumph?"

"She saved his life. But she also realizes she can't be with him. So yes and no."

"So it's not so clear."

"It's *never* clear," she said.

We watched the next movie, another old classic, this one a slap-stick comedy, Joany gradually sinking onto the floor, me stretching out on the futon. When it ended, Joany walked to the TV to flip it off, turned back and stretched, reaching her arms straight overhead, then bending forward to touch her toes, arching her back as she gripped each leg, touching chin to knee.

"Nobody triumphed in that one," I said.

"Just because it's a comedy doesn't mean it's not serious," she said, straightening. "You know," she said, "laughing to keep from crying?"

"Why can't it just be funny? Just plain funny with no hidden misery?"

"Is that what you'd like?" She tilted her head side to side, keeping her eyes on me.

"What?" I said, but she kept staring. "What?" I said again, and she slowly blinked, breaking the spell, and took her mug to the kitchen, stopping on her way back to flip through some magazines on a shelf.

"Going to bed?" I asked.

She nodded without looking up from her search.

"I'm glad you were here tonight," I said, and she turned to me, her eyes softening.

"I'm glad too," she said. Then she pirouetted on one foot and walked up the stairs.

I glided home along dark roads twisting through woods until I reached the potato fields in Amagansett where the sky opened out above, lit with stars. I slid down through the apple orchard and past the golf course, crossed the tracks, and headed down Atlantic Avenue to Bluff Road.

Inside, on the kitchen table lay a post-card picturing a pelican, from Tessy. In boxy, printed letters she said the weather was wonderful, she had a year-round flower garden, and a couple leads for a job as a waitress. "The apartment is too small for three of us," she wrote, "but I want you to know, Ricky, I'm trying."

Chapter 9

JANUARY, '84, THE last game of the season was against our rival, Southampton, a game we needed to win to make the county playoffs. Since mid-season I'd been a starter, Ben's time steadily decreasing until the last three games in which he didn't play at all, just sat brooding at the end of the bench, not saying a word to anybody.

Because the Southampton gym was booked for an evening event, the game started at twelve o'clock Saturday afternoon, and we got off to a terrible start, going to the half down by twenty. We fought back in the second half, coming to within three points with two minutes to go, but, caught in a game-long funk, I got beat easily by my man and forced Lance to come over and commit his fifth and final foul.

Out of desperation, Coach brought in Ben, and though we summoned a final burst, I came up short on my final two jump-shots, my legs not having any spring, and we lost by five, returning to East Hampton in silence, the bus ride oddly morose because it was still daytime.

At the school, the coaches and driver got off but the rest of us sat in place, until finally Lance stood up.

"Well boys," he said, turning at the front of the bus to face us, "life . . . goes . . .fucking . . . on," and he slid down the stairs and out.

The rest of us trickled out into the late afternoon and I grabbed my bike, pulling on gloves and hat, temperature in the 40s, and pedaled through the village and along the ocean down an empty Further Lane.

A note on the table said Dad and Gladys had gone up island to visit Gladys' brother, and there was hamburger meat in the fridge and vegetables in the freezer. Instead, I guzzled a pitcher of orange juice and, ignoring the "Do not touch" post-it on the box, polished off half a peach pie.

I strolled through the house, looking out the windows of each room, at the maple trees casting long shadows across the amber grass, at the stand of scrub oak in the side yard, now bare of leaves, and through them to the next house down the road. Upstairs, I gazed out at the fields of tall brown grass out back where three new houses were coming up on flag lots.

The frustration of the loss and my half-assed play gnawing at me, my reserves of energy scarcely tapped, I pulled on my work boots and searched for something heavy to put in my windbreaker pockets. My five-pound barbell weights wouldn't fit so it was back down to the kitchen where I grabbed two cans of tomato sauce and two large cans of baked beans. Stuffing one can of beans and one of sauce in each pocket, I bounced in place and the cans bounced against my thighs, so I wound a piece of twine over the windbreaker around my waist, anchoring the cans in place, and headed for the beach.

The wind out of the east, I started off running into it, toward Napeague in the soft sand near the dunes. The twine loosening, cans coming loose, I removed the two cans of beans from windbreaker pockets and continued on, one in each hand. When I reached Big House I was moving slowly in the soft sand but, knowing the return with the wind would be easier, pushed it to the last house on the stretch.

Running back with the wind, my strides longer than the footprints of my approach, beads of sweat slid down my scalp. As my breathing loosened, I picked up the pace and pushed into a sprint for the final two hundred yards.

As I paced in the parking lot, cooling down, two pickups pulled up, Wesley and Jason, parking several spaces apart facing the sea.

Wesley rolled down his window, his face tired, unshaven. Behind him in the back, Guts peered out, tail thumping the side.

"What'd you find?" Wesley said.

I looked at the beans in my hands. "Already had 'em."

"Beans?"

"Extra weight. I'm working out."

"S'pose it's better than eating them bastards."

Jason rolled down his passenger window. "What the hell you got?"

"Beans," Wesley said. "He's running with goddam beans."

"You been *running?*" Jason said.

"For basketball," I said.

"'Case they change the rules," Wesley said, "and make everybody wear workboots and carry two cans of beans."

Jason smiled and shook his head.

"Thought you had a game today," Wesley said.

"We did. Lost to Southampton."

"That the last one?"

"Yeah."

Wesley looked back at the ocean, squinting, and asked, "Ben play?"

"Just a few minutes," I said. "Sometimes I wonder if Coach realizes how good he is."

"Good," Wesley said, "but pig-headed."

"Still, since I joined the team, Coach—"

"Coach nothing," Wesley said, looking at me with hardened eyes. "Ben's had a chip on his shoulder since I can remember. Why you think he don't fish? Because he'd have to work *with* somebody."

Wesley looked back at the ocean, the tendon in his jaw moving as he ground his teeth.

"So how's the fishing?" I said.

"Suppose somewhere it's good."

I wondered if the poor fishing was because it got worse in the winter or because of the new laws restricting the size of the haul, protecting the fish supply for sportsmen.

"You better get your behind into a warm shower," Wesley said.

"I guess." I reached into the back and patted Guts.

"Take care ya bastard," Wesley said. "Dunk one for the haul-seiners."

"Dunk a can of beans," Jason called over.

They each rolled up their window, returning their eyes to the sea, and I jogged up the hill toward home.

A week or so after the Southampton game, I biked to the Williams' and, when Joany answered the door, asked if Lance was home, though I knew he was up-island for the all-county awards banquet.

Joany let me in and the first thing she said was, "I want to learn that trick I saw you do before the game."

"Missing a lay-up?" I said.

"You had the ball going around your arms." She held her arms in a circle and rolled them.

I went up to Lance's room to find a basketball and, returning, positioned myself behind Joany, reaching around her to clasp her wrists and undulate her arms beneath the circling ball.

Joany shrieked with pleasure when the ball completed a circle and rolled off, then she made me demonstrate, studying closely, her face amused but intent, and we tried again.

With each attempt, I eased my body tighter against hers, until my chest was firm against her back, the side of my face brushing hers, and when the ball again rolled off, I held her in place, feeling her silky sweater beneath my chin.

"Ricky?"

"Yeah?"

"What are you doing?" Her voice reverberated against my chest.

"Holding you."

"You're my brother's best friend," she said, stepping out from my grasp. "I'd never do that to Lance."

"Do what?"

She shook her head. "You don't understand," she said, and walked off.

"Joany."

At the doorway she spun back. "You're the first friend he's had, Ricky—outside Freetown."

Joany walked briskly from the room and I heard quick steps on the stairs.

I stood in the kitchen hoping she'd return, then sat waiting at the counter as the daylight waned. Finally, I rode home along Town Lane, speeding in the near dark past two chasing dogs, on past the potato fields and through the orchard, not a single car passing, nothing after the dogs to distract me from the mishap in Joany's kitchen. Jesus Christ, I thought, I finally get the nerve to put my arms around her and I'm committing an act of betrayal.

At home, the only light on was in Tessy's vacant room. I ran up the stairs and poked my head in the doorway, Tessy turning from her suitcase, opened on the bed.

"You're back," I said, but when I walked over and hugged her she hardly hugged back.

"It's like she's not even a Hawkins anymore," she said.

Tessy lifted a sweater from the suitcase and carried it limp at her side to the dresser.

"They both work at this bar, alternating shifts," she said, "and the one who's home never talks about the other one." She sniffed a sweatshirt and tossed it in the corner.

"Lately, Lonnie was hardly even coming home," she said, transporting a single t-shirt across the room. "And Carter, he'd just sit there in front of the TV. For hours. Lonnie would come home, go through his pockets for cigarettes, and he wouldn't even blink. Then she'd head back out."

She paused before the window then returned to the suitcase, sifting through the clothes.

"One night I fell asleep in their room because Carter was sitting out there on the couch. I wake up and he's standing next to the bed." Tessy turned and faced me. "'What's going on around here,' he says. 'Tell me what's going on.' I get up and start walking out to the living room but he stops me. 'Just tell me what's going on,' he says. "'Nothing,' I say, and he grabs my arm, but softly, like he's afraid of hurting me. 'No, no, it's okay,' he says, 'just tell me what's going on. Where's Lonnie?'

"Ricky, he looked so pitiful I started feeling sorry for him. 'Carter,' I said, 'nothing's going on,' and he grabbed my other arm like he just needed to hold on to somebody and, Ricky, it started feeling good, and he started telling me how lonely he was . . ." Tessy trailed off and turned away.

"Can you imagine doing that?" she said after a pause, turning back to me with wide uncomprehending eyes. "To my own sister? To the one person who'd helped me, who'd brought me down there in the first place?" She turned back to the window. "So I grabbed my things before she came home and hitched to the airport. I had just enough money to pay for the plane to New York and train ticket home."

Suitcase empty, Tessy closed it and placed it in the closet.

"What about you?" she said. "How's everything here?"

"Fine," I said.

"Tell me about basketball."

"Since when do you care about basketball?"

"Since now. Tell me."

So I told her about the last game, the outlook for the seniors, Higgins and Battle not eligible to graduate, but Henclik receiving a scholarship to a junior college in Pennsylvania, and Lance's only Division One offer from some religious school in the midwest, though he got plenty of offers from Division Two schools.

"We've decided to go to the same school," I said, "Bryant University in Rhode Island. Lance has a full scholarship and I'll be a walk-on."

"I'm sorry," Tessy said.

"I only played one year," I said.

"I mean because I left you here alone. All you've had is basketball."

"Basketball's plenty," I said.

"Well I'm back." Tessy looked around the room, sizing it up.

"You going back to school?" I asked.

"We'll make this place homey, Ricky. You'll be glad I'm back."

"I *am* glad."

"I can make curtains. And we'll get some plants, and a couple of space heaters for up here to make it warm. What's wrong?"

"You need to go back to school, Tessy."

"Home comes first, Ricky."

But it felt like she was playing house.

"What's wrong?" Tessy said again.

"I'm just thinking."

"It's got to be good here, Ricky."

"It'll be fine," I said. "Everything'll be fine.

Chapter 10

T HE DOME OF late-winter gray gradually thinned
and dissipated, revealing the soft blue sky of early
spring. The maple beside my window sprouted buds,
its lithe, freshly juiced branches bending deep in the wind
off the ocean. Before school, I would often bike to the beach
and watch the Bristers who had begun again hauling seine.

On this day, though the ocean appeared flat and blue
from Bluff Road, at the beach I found sets of large waves
pulsing in against an offshore wind.

Down the beach, Wesley sat in his truck watching Jason
and Petey who stood in the surf holding the dory, waiting
for a calm spell before pushing out. Another quarter mile
up the beach sat Duff's truck.

"Back at it?" I said, approaching Wesley's truck, his
window rolled down.

Wesley glanced at me and returned his eyes to the two
in the surf. "Where's your beans?" he said.

"Ate 'em."

Jason and Petey timed their surge with the backwash
and rode swiftly through the breakers, the nose of the boat
rising into the air as they sped over the cresting waves and

out to sea where Jason dumped the seine over the side and Petey, in the back, steered them in a broad arc.

On their way in, they stopped beyond the breakers, Petey standing and peering back at the incoming waves, watching for a lull. Once the last wave of a large set had passed beneath the hull, he sat and gunned the motor. The boat surged forward, then sputtered and coughed. Petey wrenched the choke handle back and forth but the motor stalled, and he yanked the cord hard three times but got no response. Petey hammered his fist once against the metal casing and, at the same moment as Wesley called out *"Row,"* reached into the boat for the oars, thrust them in the oarlocks, and began rowing. A small wave pushed beneath them as he pulled the oars, circling them up and slapping them back down, with a larger wave surging in.

Petey managed to get the boat in ahead of the crashing wave, the force of its crash bouncing the boat but not rolling it. Then they bogged down in the white water, Petey continuing to row, Jason jumping out to pull as the next wave crested behind them. But the surf was higher than Jason expected, his chest-high waders filling with water, anchoring him in place, and as Petey rowed the boat to safety, Jason was caught beneath the crashing wave.

Already out of the truck, Wesley pulled off his boots, me beside him pulling off my sneakers, and we dove into the icy surf where there was no sign of Jason. Stepping through the waist-high water, pulling ourselves with our hands, Jason's head appeared, and another wave broke just as we reached him, burying us all. Numb and gasping for air, I lifted my head free of the settling water and saw

Wesley with a hold of Jason's arm. I grabbed Jason's other arm, and we dragged him and his waders filled with water slowly to shore, where Jason flopped down on his back, water pouring from his waders back to sea.

"That was about bright," Petey said, the dory safely beached.

Chest heaving, Jason lay on his back staring at the sky. "I didn't know it was so deep," he said.

"You're goddam half out to sea!" Wesley yelled, turning and glaring, first at Jason, then Petey. "Ain't either of you got the goddam sense of a jackrabbit?"

Wesley turned and walked back to his truck, and Petey slapped me on the back, saying with a wink, "Sure don't see no jackrabbits hauling seine."

I helped Petey hook the dory and the nets to the winch, Jason now sitting up, hands across knees, staring out at the pounding ocean.

When they got the net in, it was nearly empty, five or six blues, a couple of sea robins, and a sand shark.

"Lot of good you are," Petey said, lifting the three-foot shark by the tail, the fish whipping its body side to side as he stepped toward me. "Say hello to Ricky here." The shark swung toward me, and I jumped back.

"Ain't shit for bass," Jason said, rejoining us, and Petey heaved the shark into the water, then each of the sea robins.

Wesley nudged the toe of his boot through the remaining fish, and gazed blankly at Jason, nodding slightly, as if getting wise to a prank.

Nobody said a word as they tossed the blues into the truck and loaded the last of the nets. I climbed in the back of Wesley's truck with Guts and when Wesley slid out at the parking lot to switch the axles back to two-wheel drive, hopped out and grabbed my bike.

"Wasn't you I was yelling at," Wesley said.

"I know," I said.

"But this is no time to be fooling around," he said. "Not with this amount of fish." He rotated the last hub and stood up. "Ben moved in with his uncle over in Wainscott," he said. "You seen him around?"

"No," I said. "Didn't know he moved."

"Well, if you see him, tell him to come by and say hello to his family."

Wesley reached a foot in the cab, but before getting in, turned his head and peered off at the ocean.

"You are one merciless son of a bitch," he said, and climbed in the truck.

With the arrival of Memorial Day and the warming weather, more and more people flowed out onto the East End and into the House of Dogs. The owner offered me a full schedule and I began a routine of finishing the dinner dishes around eleven, taking over the hamburger grill till twelve, then changing into clean jeans and T-shirt and strolling out to the bar, where the owner allowed a few of us to hang out on condition that those of us who were underage didn't drink, though he soon lost track, drinking age in June of '84 still 18.

One Friday after I'd sprayed down the grill, I found Higgins leaning against the wall in the dim light between the bar and juke box. He wore a gold Lakers cap backwards and held a beer in two fingers.

"What's up, Higgins?"

"Coolin, man."

Battle came out of the bathroom, dark arms glistening beneath a white tank-top.

"What's happening, Battle?" I said.

"Alright, man."

"Coolin like your boy here?" I said.

He glanced at Higgins. "Shit," he said, retrieving his beer from the ledge over the bathroom door.

I continued on through the crowd, found Ben, who was 18, seated at the bar. I sat beside him and ordered a beer.

"Your old man was asking for you," I said.

"Oh yeah?"

"Said you should stop by the house."

"Suppose I should."

"Where you been?" I said. "Haven't seen you since the season ended."

"Working mostly. My uncle I moved in with's a builder." He turned and faced me. "Donna won't even talk to me," he said.

"Maybe you're better off," I said.

"So I should just say fuck it?"

I nodded and Ben eyed himself in the mirror behind the bar, took a long swallow, looked from his reflection to mine.

"Then that's what I'll do," Ben said, "tell her to go fuck herself," and he stood up and walked out, heading, I assumed, to the phone booth outside.

In a few minutes, Ben returned and downed the last of his beer without sitting down.

"I keep getting her answering machine," he said.

"So?"

"Then I'll tell her to her face."

"Right now?"

"I got to, Ricky. I can't keep driving around all night. I'll fucking go crazy." He took a step away and stopped. "Can you keep a secret?" he said, eyeing me, his lips pushing into a crooked smile. I nodded. "I ain't staying with no uncle. I just been sleeping any place." He stepped away and again stopped.

"And no hard feelings about basketball," he said. "Game's not meant for white people anyway."

I watched him march from the bar, took a long pull off my beer, and sauntered back to Higgins and Battle.

"Look at you," Battle said.

"What?" I said.

"Like you own the place."

"Like you Cool Motion," Higgins said. "Can't nothin' in the world touch you."

"It's summertime," I said.

"That you?" Battle said. "Cool Motion?"

I tipped my bottle back and drained it. "That's me," I said. "Who needs one?"

The bartender gave me a free round and when I delivered the beers Higgins and Battle were talking about Ben.

"The boy is sour," Battle said.

"He's more than sour," I said, almost telling them what he'd just said but deciding against it. "Heart-broken," I said. "Donna dumped him."

We drank our beers and watched the new arrivals parade past on their way out to the back deck. A dark Black girl wearing a pink crew-neck sweater, matching socks, and penny loafers came in with a bunch of white friends, and Higgins stepped in front of her.

"Bout time you got here," he said, smiling.

"Do I know you?" she said.

"Course you do," Higgins said, gesturing at Battle. "We the only two brothers in here."

"Not *my* brothers," she said, and followed her friends out to the deck.

Higgins turned back to us, shaking his head, and he and Battle finished their beers and said they were going to McClain's, a Black club in Mattituck, the other side of Southampton. We exchanged high-fives, and they left.

I leaned back against the wall, the bass from the jukebox vibrating into my back, and watched the door, hoping to see Joany.

Giving up on the door, I took a stool at the bar for one last beer. Gazing at myself in the mirror, a figure appeared at my shoulder, Tessy, holding her coat closed with both hands.

"It's almost two o'clock," I said.

"Lonnie called," she said. "Something's wrong, Ricky. One minute she's telling me she needs a doctor and the next minute she's talking about Christmas, wanting you and me to go to Florida."

"Probably drunk," I said.

"It was something else," Tessy said. "She kept saying, 'This fucking place,' 'this fucking place,' but when I asked what place, she just changed the subject."

I shook my head and looked around at the thinning crowd.

"I called the apartment," Tessy said, "but there was no answer. Ricky, we have to do something."

I walked my bike beside Tessy through the intermittent cones of light on Main Street, onto Atlantic Avenue, and turned the corner onto Bluff Road.

As we walked upstairs, I assured her we'd call Lonnie the next day to get the details, then headed back out into the night.

Beer buzz gone flat, too tired to return to the Dog House, I headed toward the beach, needing some cool air. But the breeze off the water wasn't refreshing, the June air already thick with humidity, the emptiness of winter crowded away by music and weekenders and the murky numbness of beer.

My eyes adjusting to the moonless night, the beach a shade lighter than the water, I walked slowly along the shore, breathing as deeply as I could.

A week later, Lonnie finally responded to the daily messages Tessy and I had been leaving on her answering machine, calling to say she'd spent six days in jail.

"I got beat up so bad I could hardly walk, but did they take me to the hospital?" she said, Tessy and I standing together in the kitchen holding our ears to the phone. "No. They threw me in a paddy wagon and locked me up."

"Are you okay?" I asked her.

"I'm fine," Lonnie said with a huff. "It's the world that's going to shit."

Chapter 11

SATURDAY NIGHT, LAST weekend of June, we closed
the grill early, out of hamburger, and I headed out
to the bar, crowd still light, jazz piano plinking the
air from speakers above the rows of liquor bottles. Behind
me, people sat at tables strewn with glasses and crumpled
napkins, beside me at the bar two couples and a guy by
himself.

I gazed into the mirror as the first beer eased into my
blood, washing away the self-consciousness of sitting alone,
and before I could ask, the bartender threw me a wink and
another beer. At the door, the trickle of people gradually
thickened into a steady stream, until the doorway filled
with the hulking body of Henclik.

Henclik sat beside me, ordered himself a beer and a
7-Up for Ben, trailing along behind.

"Fuck you," Ben said, catching up, seeing the drink, and
ordering himself a beer.

"This bonacker's on a mission," Henclik said.

"Bonacker?" Ben said.

"Bonacker, bubby, whatever."

"A bonacker's from East Hampton. I'm from Lazy Point."

Henclik slapped his back with a thick open hand. "Congratulations!"

"Fuck you," Ben said, taking a long chug from his beer.

I ordered another and strolled back to the jukebox, turned on at 11, dropped in a few quarters, selected some songs, turned to see Lance and, trailing behind him, Joany, wearing a woolen hat, black sweats, and a navy pea coat—in June. Lance and I high-fived, and he stepped over to the bar.

"Damn," I said to Joany.

"What?" she said.

"It's been a while."

"I've been busy," she said.

"Art?"

"Oh, I'm working on some projects."

"I've been busy too," I said, but she didn't show any interest. "What brings you here?" I said.

"Why?"

I sipped my beer. "Listen," I said, "you look nice."

She peered into the glass casing of the jukebox.

"I mean it," I said, "you look, I don't know, *warm.*"

"You kidding me?" she said, spinning the wheel, flipping through the selections. "Neil Diamond?"

"Come," I said, and led her out to the back deck where we found a table in the far corner. We ordered beers from the waitress and watched the competition between three guys at the next table for the attention of the lone woman, sharp-featured with a crew-cut and a loose T-shirt, sleeves torn off. Our beers came and Joany fiddled with hers, gazing at it without drinking.

"It's good to see you," I said.

"Is it?" she said.

"Joany," I said.

"You're the one that just disappeared."

"You told me to."

She carved a fingernail down through the wet label. "Do you always do that?" she said. "As soon as there's a little bump, disappear?"

"You can see me now, can't you?" I said.

Joany didn't respond and we sat quietly, each of us peeling our labels, Joany's in even strips, mine one corner at a time, carefully preserving the whole.

By the time I finished the beer, I was feeling buzzed, giddy, and told Joany I'd be right back. I found Higgins at the bar with a Dog House regular, a guy from the city named Henry, and they bought me a round and we clinked bottles and drank.

Then I remembered Joany and cruised back out to the deck where she sat in the same place gazing up at the canopy of foliage.

"Sorry," I said.

"What's so funny?" she said.

"Nothing." But the buzz from the beer, along with Joany's presence, kept me smiling.

"Lance out there?" she said. "I better be going."

"Don't," I said, but Joany stood up and went inside.

I followed to see her take the keys from Lance, then to the front door where I watched her walk down the ramp and onto the sidewalk.

"Joany!" I called, and she turned back. But I didn't know what to say.

I held a hand out to either side. "Can you see me now?" I said.

Joany shook her head and walked off.

Ben was gone but Lance and Henclik were in the alcove, Henclik spotting a girl he'd met the week before, exhaling a long stream of air, and making his move.

"Boy drinks a couple of beers and look at him," Lance said. "Like he's Johnny Smooth."

The beer kept flowing and we rounded up Higgins and Henry for shots of tequila, offering one to a woman at the bar with thick black hair brushed straight back and a black dress with thin straps. Higgins and I told her we were trying to decide where to play ball in college, UCLA or North Carolina.

"I *might* go straight to the pros," Higgins said. But the woman, Carla, was busy preparing her lemon and salt.

She downed her shot and fished through her purse, setting a twenty on the bar for another round and, when she laughed, pressed one hand against her stomach and threw her other around whoever was closest.

"Here's to East Hampton," she said, "*finally.*"

We clinked shot glasses and drank.

"I mean," Carla said, shouting over the noise, "Summer finally comes and where am I? Stuck in fucking Manhattan."

"I heard that," Higgins said. "Who you with?"

"Nobody." She took a sip from my beer, eyeing herself in the mirror behind the bar. "Absolutely nobody."

Carla shook her head, as if to free herself of something, and pulled out another twenty.

Lance said he was leaving, and he and I stepped away from the others.

"You sure?" I said.

"Go ahead, man, have a good time." And he slid off into the crowd.

The four of us took turns dancing with Carla, sometimes two at a time, each of us getting a slow dance, and at last call, Henry, the only one with a car, offered her a ride and walked her out clinging to his arm.

Higgins and Battle bummed a ride out front, and I retrieved my bike from the back and pedaled home, riding in as straight a line as possible.

The next day, after sleeping till noon, I met up with my father in the kitchen. I'd hardly seen him since our talk about roasted chicken.

He glanced at the clock. "Life sure is tough for you kids," he said.

"Not really," I said.

He released a short puff of laughter. "Oh yes it is," he said. "Going out every night, spending the day at the beach, playing basketball . . . I don't know how you do it."

"Is that what you think, all I do is party and play basketball?"

"You do have a job, I'll give you credit for that. But how much money have you saved?"

The truth was I'd been saving most of what I earned, but I felt baited. "There's more to life than saving money," I said.

"Like what?" he said, squinting at me. "What's so important that it's worth sacrificing your future for?"

I stood there looking at him, feelings and thoughts swirling together, but had no words.

I found Tessy in the garden, yanking weeds between splayed knees, wearing panther-eye sunglasses, and a gold wristwatch that glinted in the thick August sunlight.

"They're Mom's," she said, removing the glasses. "And this is the watch she promised me. Grandma's, from Stockholm. I found them in the attic. There's clothes, a jewelry box . . ."

"Tessy," I said, "are you getting along with him?"

She answered quickly, as if expecting the question. "You have to accept him for who he is."

"Why?" I said.

"Because he's your father."

"Suppose your father's Hitler?"

"It's blood, Ricky. It's all we have."

"Maybe it's all you have," I said.

"Maybe it is," she said.

"Tessy, it's not."

She pulled sullenly at the weeds. "You only get one father," she said.

I knelt beside her. "I know Florida didn't work out, but there's life beyond this place, beyond this house, Tessy."

"I'm happy here," she said.

"Fine," I said, rising, "spend your life pulling weeds."

I grabbed my ball and biked to the court, first time in weeks, and started out shooting jumpers. Missing more than I made, I dribbled the length of the court and tried to dunk but couldn't. Soon I was winded but, still determined, tried again to dunk but still couldn't.

"Yo, Cool." Lance had pulled up in Jackie's car. "Out here with all your friends?"

"The hell with this," I said, and walked over and got in the car. "What's up, superstar?"

"Tanya's father died," he said, and we drove in silence to Indian Wells, pulling up to the ocean, deep blue, flecked with white caps.

"It's like she's falling," Lance said, "and I don't know what to do."

"She leave?"

"Yeah. I'm going tomorrow. Check it out," he said, turning and looking at me. "I'm all she's got."

We drove along the back roads, stopping at each beach, Lance shutting off the motor at Georgica where we watched soupy waves splash against the shore.

"Summertime," Lance said, "sum, sum, summertime."

"Few more weeks and we'll be gone," I said.

"Yeah," Lance said.

"We've got a choice of bus or train," I said.

"Right," Lance said. "Check out the gulls." Offshore, a group of seagulls were circling and diving down at what looked to be a thick log.

"Looks like Henclik," Lance said, and we walked down to the water, the object, a tree trunk or maybe part of a boat, floating a hundred or so yards offshore.

"What is it?" I said.

"Henclik. Must have fell asleep and the tide came in."

Gulls continued lining up in the sky, diving and lighting on one end that rose up from the water until being replaced by the next, and swooping out in a circle to the end of the line.

"Yo, Lance," I said, "seriously. How we going to get up to Bryant?"

"Ricky," he said, "we'll get there, okay?"

We trailed after the floating log as it drifted along without coming closer to shore, then walked back to the car and drove in silence to Lance's.

We sat at the counter before a bag of chips and salsa, and Joany walked in wearing a purple T-shirt and checkered boxers. Avoiding my eyes, she removed an orange from the fridge, walked to the window, stood for a moment gazing out, and left the room.

Lance said he had to go water Tanya's plants, and headed out the kitchen door, poking his head back in.

"You cool?" he said.

I nodded, and he shut the door.

I found Joany upstairs on the bed in Jackie's room flipping through a magazine.

"Sorry about last night," I said.

"Where's Lance?" she said.

"Once we got partying, everything got so, you know
. . ."

"He leave?"

"Yes." I sat in the wicker chair across from her.
"Everything okay with you?"

"Don't play games, Ricky."

"Do I have a choice? Every time I come over you act
so—"

"Then don't come over."

"You see?"

Her eyes hardened. "I'm not going to let you play with
me, Ricky."

"I'm not playing."

We continued to stare at each other, until finally her
eyes softened and she lowered them. I moved to the edge
of the bed.

"What is it?" I said.

"Nothing." She flipped another page.

"Last night," I said, "you finally come to the Dog
House—what I've been hoping for all summer—and it felt
so good, I don't know, it was like it felt too good."

Joany lifted her eyes, and I leaned over and kissed her
cheek. She studied me, blinking slowly, and I kissed her
forehead.

As I moved onto the bed, Joany kept studying me. She
didn't resist, just watched as I kissed her mouth. I kissed her
again, my lips pushing beneath hers for the moist underside,
and she fell slowly back, eyes open, until her head reached

the pillow and I stared down at the disappointment that lay like lead in her eyes.

"What's wrong?" I said.

Joany spun her legs off the bed, facing away.

"You want me to leave?" I said.

"Yes," she said.

Chapter 12

BY THE TIME Lance showed up at the Dog House, it was nearly midnight. He was looking down, so I asked how Tanya was doing.

"She's fine," he said.

"What's Joany up to?" I said.

"I don't know, doing shit."

"She stay home tonight?"

"You so interested, Cool, why you asking me?" He turned and walked to the jukebox.

I finished my can of Coke and joined him. "You're right," I said. "I should ask her."

"There you go."

"Something wrong?" I asked.

"Nope."

"Talk about me not speaking my mind."

Lance looked up at me. "I'm going to Pennsylvania tomorrow, and it's just, I don't know, like I've got no choice."

"Then don't go," I said.

"It's not that I don't want to. I mean, her father just died."

"So what's the problem?"

"I keep getting pulled in deeper."

"Then put it in reverse," I said. "Back out."

"I don't want to back out. Are you listening?" Lance glared at me, then looked away. "I wish you'd see that it's possible to do something and still not like it."

"Okay," I said, "I hear you," and offered Lance a fist, which he bumped.

"Speaking of doing the right thing," I said, "I better go see your sister."

Lance's eyes for the first time showed a little life. "How you know she's home?" he said.

"Guess I don't."

Lance gave me a wink, said "Good luck," and I headed out to my bike and on through the night to Freetown.

My knock got no response so I walked in, calling Hello from the kitchen and moving into the living room where Joany sat coated in the light from the television.

"I'm back," I said, sitting beside her.

She didn't respond.

"You going to talk?" I said.

"It's a news special about Guatemala."

"Joany." I stood up and still she didn't look so I turned to leave.

"Just walk away," she said.

"Last night you told me to, and now you're not talking."

"Last night, Ricky, you were like some sort of robot."

"Are you going to talk to me?"

"What do you call this?" But she kept staring at the set.

"I didn't even think you'd be here," I said. "Lance said you were out doing shit."

"Good for him."

"Then what are you mad at? And if you're so busy, why are you sitting home watching television?"

"I just got home. And who says I'm mad?"

I stepped toward her and saw dishes on the floor beside the futon. "Whose dishes?"

"How should I know?" she said, but had to purse her lips to suppress a smile.

"Joany, I'm *glad* you're here."

She looked down at the dishes. "Probably Trip's."

"Joany."

"I'm serious," she said, throwing me a glance.

I sat beside her.

"When you come over," she said, "and start coming on to me completely out of the blue, how am I supposed to react?"

"Sometimes I don't know how to approach you," I said. "So I just took a chance."

"Go slower and it'll be less chancy," she said.

A movie came on and we lay together on the futon, Joany predicting a few scenes then climbing on my back and massaging my neck and shoulders.

"Jesus," she said, digging her fingers into the muscles. "Feels like steel cable."

"Partying's hard work," I said.

She ran a knuckle down either side of my spine. "What's wrong with staying home once in a while?" I didn't answer and she continued. "Lance said your house is depressing, said he invited you to stay here."

"My sister would go crazy if I left her alone."

Joany gave my back a pat, and I rolled over beneath her. She pinned my hands back against the mattress, lowered her face to within a few inches of mine.

"Now what are you going to do?" she said.

"Whatever you say," I said.

Her knees tightened on my hips. "Tell me about Ricky Hawkins," she said.

"Just some dude, plays a little ball, hangs out."

"And?"

"He lives in Amagansett, with a sister, father, and step-mother."

"The sister's Tessy," Joany said, "because Lonnie's in Florida. Go on."

I made a weak effort to free my arms.

"What happened to your mother?" Joany said.

"Died of cancer."

"When?"

"Two years ago."

"And your father remarried?"

"The summer after she died, he brought a woman from work to move in with us. Gladys."

"You get along with her?"

"She's there for my father, not us."

"But she moved in with all of you."

"It's like there's two separate families, parents and kids."

"What about your sisters?" Joany said. "They feel the same way?"

"We all pretty much fend for ourselves."

"But you said your sister wouldn't like it if you stayed here. That's not fending for herself."

"Maybe not, but with Tessy, it's like . . . "

Joany waited a moment. "Like what?" she said.

"Like she's stuck in a bubble."

"Maybe she needs time," Joany said.

Joany brought out two large mugs of tea, clicked off the television, and we sat up on the futon facing each other.

"Your turn," I said. "What happened to your father?"

Joany pulled in a deep breath and slowly released it. "He went off to amass his fortune—seven years ago."

Joany stared past me, her mind scrolling back. "We hadn't seen him for a few months," she said. "Then he came out from the city in the middle of the week, no holiday, just a weekday afternoon. I come in from school and he's standing in the kitchen with my mother. Then Lance and Trip come in and he sits us all down in the living room and gives us presents. *Presents.*" Joany shook her head, staring past me. "He gave Lance tickets for the Knicks, and that was okay, but then he gave Tripoli his book of sketches and gave me his mother's ring, and it was so weird, like he was handing us our inheritance.

"So he gets up to leave and Tripoli, who's four, starts screaming and grabbing onto his leg. He said he was just going back to work, but Tripoli wouldn't let go, and Lance just stood there trying to be so strong. Then I started crying and my father comes over and says, 'I'm just going back to New York.'

"As soon as he left, Jackie started cooking—that's what she does. Lance went up to his room, and I sat down here with Tripoli, who was crying so hard he could barely breathe, and I kept telling him, 'He'll be back, Daddy'll be back.'"

Joany gazed around the room, letting the scene finish itself, then slowly swung her head around and looked at me.

"What is it about men," she said, "that they can't face their own children?"

Lance came in about three, waking us. "See you two found each other," he said.

"You're staying here tonight?" Joany said to him.

Lance sank into the easy chair. "I'm taking Trip for sneakers tomorrow morning before I go to Pennsylvania. Tanya call?"

"I was out," Joany said, looking at me and smiling. "Really. We went to eat."

Lance lifted himself out of the chair, kissed Joany on the cheek, and gave me a sleepy high-five. "I told you she'd be here," he said.

"You said she was out."

"Did I? Damn." Lance walked slowly up the stairs. "Y'all be good," he said.

Joany and I watched a movie, until her eyes began to fall closed. Knowing I was watching her, she smiled, lifted my arm and slid beneath it, burrowing in against me.

I woke into the grey light of the television, muted it with the remote, and pondered Joany's sleeping face, blank and trusting in the soft light. I kissed her softly on the cheek and moved toward her lips.

Only once our mouths were joined did Joany open her eyes, the delicate brown of her irises visible in the dim light. She pulled her face away but held her eyes on mine.

"Ricky?" she whispered.

"Yes?" I said, gazing down at her.

A shudder moved through her body and her eyes squinted but didn't close.

"I swore I would never let this happen," she said.

"Let what happen?"

Her arms tightened around my back and her eyes clenched closed as she pulled me tight against her. *"This,"* she said.

Although I'd hardly slept, I biked home in tenth gear the whole way, flying down Town Lane, past the apple orchard and golf course, barely slowing to cross the highway onto Atlantic Avenue. For although there'd been a couple of awkward moments, we'd fumbled through them together, and waking in the morning, kissing Joany's sleeping face, and heading out into the August morning, everything felt different.

I found Tessy in the garden, the low sun silhouetting her legs through the white cotton dress as she leaned back on one hand, knees up, and dabbed at the soil with the other. She wore neither the watch nor sunglasses.

"Hit the beach, Tess?"

"Here in the garden, I'm connected. Why would I want to go to the beach?"

I sat down on the strip of grass between the plots of soil. "You okay?"

She nodded slowly. "I'm wonderful," she said airily.

"Me too," I said, hoping she'd ask why.

"I can hear God, you know," she said. "His voice comes into me. Just now, before you came, he told me Mom was fine. Then she told me herself. She wants you to know too."

"Okay," I said.

"It's like this whole other world, Ricky."

"What's wrong with this one?"

"I always thought it was so unfair that she got taken away before we could really talk. But now I know we still can."

"Tessy, you don't talk to anybody here."

"It's not necessary."

"What about Dad, you been talking to him?"

"Sometimes about gardening."

"Ever talk about you?"

"Ricky, our father is very—you have to see what's important to him. Besides, once you've talked with God, other conversations aren't so important."

"Well, I'm going to the beach."

Tessy looked up at the sky. "He doesn't know any better," she said.

After changing into my suit, I walked through the yard toward the street, but seeing Tessy sitting out in the garden, turned and walked back. Once I apologized, first to Tessy, then to God, she agreed to go for a swim.

We walked down the hill into the morning fog at the shore. Tessy lifted her dress above her knees as we waded into the green-gray water, waves lurching from the thick wall of fog and crashing before us, Tessy clasping my hand as the spray soaked through her dress. We waded out until a wall of water appeared and dove, Tessy resurfacing like an otter, nose straight up, water sliding from her face.

"You see?" I said. "This world isn't so bad."

Tessy grinned, then pounced on me, pushing me under, and I resurfaced to see a large wave climbing through the fog and we both dove, emerging to a calm spell, the sun warming our faces and shoulders as it burned through the haze.

"Ricky," Tessy said, wrapping herself in a towel, "what if you found something that belonged to somebody you really loved, and somebody took it from you? Would they be wrong for taking it?"

"Taking what?"

"Something special that was hers, or his, and you found it and started wearing it, then somebody said it was theirs but you knew they didn't love her as much as you. Would that be wrong of them?"

"If I had the slightest clue what you were talking about . . ."

"Promise you'll be open minded."

"I promise."

"That watch of Mom's I found? Gladys said it was hers, all the stuff in the jewelry box in the attic was hers."

"It's Mom's," I said.

"Dad said he gave it to Gladys. I asked him. He said maybe it was a mistake, but it was already done." She trailed a toe through the sand. "It's no big deal. It's just that Mom got that watch from her mother, and she always told me I would get it next."

"Yeah," I said, "you're going way too far, wanting something your mother promised you."

"Sometimes I just get weak..."

"Tessy, I'm being sarcastic," I said. "Weak isn't wanting something that's yours."

"I shouldn't have told you," she said.

"Who are you trying to protect?"

"Don't get angry, Ricky."

"I don't like to be stolen from. Or for my sister to be stolen from."

"We need to forgive."

The sun, meanwhile, had burned away the haze, revealing a powder-blue sky. Small clusters of people were moving down and settling on the beach. Towel over her shoulders, Tessy's dress was drying.

"Why?" I said. "Why should we forgive them?"

"Because they don't know any better."

"What don't they know, Tessy?"

"How important it is to me."

"But you told Dad that Mom promised it to you."

"He didn't know."

"Then he doesn't need to be forgiven," I said. "He needs to be educated." I started off toward the parking lot.

"It's not like I'm a saint," she said.

I turned back. "So anybody can do whatever they want to you, because you're not perfect?"

"I'm not saying that."

"Then let's go get your watch."

"I can't stand fighting," she said.

"It's not fighting, Tessy. It's fighting *back*."

We found my father and Gladys sitting at the glass table on the back deck, a pot of coffee and plate of pastries between them. As Gladys reached for a croissant, the gold watch sparkled in the sunlight.

We ascended the steps and my father turned in his chair. "Problem?" he said.

"That's Mom's watch," I said.

"He means it used to be," Tessy said.

"She left it for Tessy," I said.

"You know that for a fact, do you?" my father said.

"Yes," I said, hands at my sides knotted into fists.

"Can we discuss this another time?" Gladys said.

"This is no discussion," I said. "Give us the watch."

"Harry," Gladys said.

"It just so happens that watch was left to me," he said.

"You're saying Mom lied to Tessy?"

"Don't put words in my mouth."

"Then you say it. Mom lied."

"That'll be enough," he said, grimacing as he reached for a roll with one hand and stabbed his knife into the bar of butter with the other.

"You take the one thing, one heirloom, Mom left for Tessy," I said, "and then you say she lied to us?"

"If you—" he began, but I cut him off.

"I'm going away in a couple of weeks," I said, "and I won't have to deal with this shit anymore, but you're not doing this to Tessy, not while you just sit out here with your—" I looked from him to Gladys, not knowing what to call her.

"You started pretty strong," he said. "Go ahead and finish."

But there was no word for the picture I saw before me— Gladys sitting there wearing Mom's watch.

"You can't do this," I said, walking around the table.

I grabbed at the watch on Gladys's wrist, Tessy trying to restrain me as Gladys stood and backed away. I felt my father's hands on my shoulders, and Tessy screamed, "Leave him alone!" pulling at my father from behind.

"Give it to me!" I said, Gladys backing against the house, her wrist raised above her head. I again demanded the watch and pinned her arm against the shingles.

In one quick motion, Gladys reached up with her free hand, yanked off the watch, and threw it down to the deck, in the next instant smashing it beneath her heel.

We all stopped still. I turned to Tessy who had my father by the arm. She gazed back at me, stunned, while my father peered at Gladys, his face stuck between expressions, as if seeing something he couldn't register.

"For God's sake," Gladys said, "he was attacking me."

Chapter 13

THE NEXT DAY, I called Joany, Trip answering, saying she'd gone up island shopping with Jackie, so I headed to the beach. Not seeing the fishermen, I walked along the shore tossing rocks into waves, trying to time the rock's entry so the wave would swallow it. I walked toward Indian Wells, selecting and tossing smooth ovals, and at Indian Wells turned and ran back through the soft sand, breathing heavily as I approached Atlantic Avenue, pushing into a sprint, my thighs growing thick, depleted of oxygen, for the final two hundred yards to the coast-guard-station-turned-snack-bar.

Walking it off in the parking lot, I saw Minkoff approaching, practicing his cross-over with an imaginary ball.

"Holy shit," I said, "you got shorter."

"Fuck you," he said, adding, "Cool Motion."

"Where'd you get that?"

"Kyle Higgins and them were at the East Hampton courts the other day. That's what they called you."

"So you're hanging in East Hampton? How do you get there?"

He mimed a jump shot. "I bum a ride with my next-door neighbor, some real estate dude. He goes to his office, and I go to mine."

"Finally got yourself some game," I said.

"Told 'em the only reason I didn't play with you and Lance and them is 'cause I have a heart problem." He closed his eyes, grabbed at his chest, and laughed.

Bobbing his hand before him as if dribbling a ball, Minkoff stuck out his butt and backed into me.

"Minkoff down low," he said, "fakes left, turns back. . ." He dipped his shoulder and spun, releasing a right-handed hook.

"Sweet," I said.

Next, he stepped back, the imaginary ball at his shoulder, and counted down, "Three. .two. . . one. . ." releasing the shot and watching. "Minkoff at the buzzer!"

Minkoff quieted and walked himself through a couple circles, head down. "I'm not kidding though," he said, "they say I should try out next year."

"Then you should."

He broke into a sheepish smile. "Come to the East Hampton court," he said. "We'll play one-on-one, no handicap."

"Alright," I said.

"I gotta meet my mom at the beach," he said, "some cousin of ours came out from the city."

"I'll see you at the courts."

"After four, every day I'm there. In my *office*. I'm better, Ricky, really—shit, here she is."

Coming down the hill, an orange station wagon plowed toward us.

"See you, Cool Motion."

Minkoff jogged toward the approaching car, his right hand bouncing at his side dribbling an invisible ball.

I walked into Amagansett village, sat on the bench in the sun and picked up the local paper, the front page featuring an article about the conflict between the Sentinels and the locals, the Sentinels pushing for a zoning law to require new homes be built on half acres, in some areas full acres, my father and Gladys, co-presidents of the Sentinels, each being quoted, my father insisting the new measure wouldn't damage but improve prospects for local families: "We've all got to focus on the long term, rather than our own immediate welfare," Gladys adding, "When it comes to the environment, there's no us and them, only us."

A cluster of shrieking seagulls moved into town, trailing a pickup that pulled over before me on the bench, Jason and Petey sliding out in hip-waders fastened with shoulder straps.

"What do you say, bub?" Jason said.

"Catching any fish?" I asked.

"Fish, shit," he said. "More liable to catch a goddammed Pope."

The gulls held at bay by Guts in the back, I stepped over and his tail started going, eight or ten bluefish strewn at his feet. I dropped the paper on the bench where I'd found it, gave his head a few strokes, and followed Petey and Jason as they clumped into the deli, the last Sunday of August, people in tennis outfits and beachwear standing in line, cradling their Sunday *New York Times* like firewood.

Jason and Petey poured coffees, plucked a magazine wrapped in plastic from the rack and joined the line.

"Yep, you got your country people . . . " Jason began.

"And your shitty people," Petey finished.

A man in wire-rimmed glasses swung around with his *Times* to see who was talking.

"Local color," Jason said, and the man turned back around.

Jason and Petey returned to the pickup, placed their coffees on the hood, stripped away the plastic covering, and stood beside the truck flipping through the magazine, forcing the nonstop stream of weekend traffic to bow out over the double yellow line. I pet Guts from the curb.

A passing car honked and Petey swung around, drawing his middle finger like a six-shooter.

Once they'd flipped from one cover to the other, Jason walked over, dropped the magazine in the trash, and they climbed in the truck.

"See you in church," Jason said, grinning through the open window, Petey beside him popping open a beer.

Still peering at me, Jason's eyes widened as he gunned the engine, lurching blindly into traffic before a skidding car.

Turning into our driveway, I passed an idling red Mustang, nodded at a guy with a beard and aviator sunglasses in the driver's seat who nodded back.

In the kitchen, Lonnie stood before an open cabinet, wearing tired-looking jeans and t-shirt, Tessy watching from across the room. Lonnie turned to me, face pale, eyes dark.

"I hear you're going to college," she said.

"Less than two weeks," I said.

"Good for you," Lonnie said. "Get out while you can."

Lonnie turned back to the cabinet, grabbed a can and placed it in a bag. Grabbing another, she paused to read the label.

"Can't even buy a name brand," she said, placing the can in the bag, opening the refrigerator, studying its contents, withdrawing a plastic container.

"Oh my God," she groaned. She opened the container and held it out, revealing something green beneath a layer of blue mold. "She can't even keep a refrigerator."

Lonnie replaced the container, lifted the jar of mayonnaise, and placed it in the bag.

A shopping bag in each hand, Lonnie stopped in the doorway. "I told Lewis we had to come up before summer ended—he's a carpenter. Told him he could make a killing out here."

"Summer's just about over," I said.

"We found a cottage out on Lazy Point," she said. "I'll have you guys to dinner. Lewis isn't so bad." She paused at the door watching us. "Okay," she said, a smile lighting her face, "he's horrible. But come anyway."

Lonnie walked out to the car, set the two bags inside the passenger window, and ran back around to Lewis' side, where he unfolded himself from behind the wheel, a tall, gangly guy with black boots and denim vest over black T-shirt, and let her slide in through his door to the passenger's seat. Then he folded himself into his seat and backed the car down the driveway.

"She met him in jail," Tessy said, gazing out at the yard and driveway, then turned back to me. "Is Lazy Point the one on the way to Springs?"

"That's Louse Point. Lazy Point's in Napeague. Where the fishermen live."

"When are you leaving?" she asked.

"Day after Labor Day," I said.

"Ricky, she didn't even want to see us," Tessy said. "Just came for food. I told her to come back when Dad was here and she got so angry, made me swear I'd never mention him again. Then she started filling those bags."

On the phone, Joany told me she was leaving the next day to visit art schools and relatives in New England, so I arranged to meet her at the park in East Hampton and headed off on my bike.

When I arrived, the sun had cooled to an orange disk above the perimeter of trees. Across the field, I saw Joany on the swings, head bowed forward, pushing herself with her feet.

Seeing my legs, she looked up and smiled, and we walked onto the thick grass of the soccer field, Joany taking my arm in both hands, matching her strides with mine.

"We do have a good fit," she said softly, more to herself than me.

Two small girls ran before us kicking and chasing a beach ball, and we continued to the edge of the park, walking alongside the pine woods in which dusk was already settling.

"It feels like we're together," Joany said softly, "but also not."

"We're together," I said.

Joany stopped and faced me. "But you're leaving soon."

"It's just college," I said. "Besides, if you end up in art school somewhere..."

"This isn't a summer fling?"

"You're the first girlfriend I've had," I said. "If anyone's being flung..."

Joany's face eased again into a smile, and we continued walking, reaching the corner of the park and turning along the border of dark trees. We passed the basketball court, empty, no sign of Minkoff, and turned and walked through the baseball field.

On a whim, I removed my arm from Joany's shoulder and sprinted ahead, turning back after fifty yards or so.

"Come on," I said, holding my arms open, making myself a wide target, "run."

Joany walked toward me.

"Run!" I called, feeling strong. "Jump into my arms!"

Joany halted, looking skeptical. "Can you handle a hundred and twenty pounds?" she called.

"Absolutely!"

She eyed me another moment, then balled her hands into fists, swung one forward, and charged, breaking into a grin, then shrieking as she leaped, flying with a hip directly into my stomach.

I wrapped my arms around her and stumbled backward, barely staying upright.

"I told you," she said, once I'd regained my balance and adjusted her body in my arms.

"*I* told *you*," I said.

Holding my bike on one side, Joany's arm on the other, we strolled in silence through the village, the clothing boutiques displaying dummies dressed in autumn corduroys and tweeds, others with window displays of antiques, jewelry—a few locally-run stores mixed in, all shaded by the towering, two-hundred-year-old Main Street elms.

We walked through town and beneath the underpass onto Three Mile Harbor Road, which led to Freetown. Hearing a bell behind us, we stepped aside to let pass a train of four or five children on bicycles hurrying home before dark.

Outside her door, Joany stepped into my arms, said she'd be gone for two weeks, and promised to call first thing upon her return.

I felt an ease with her, a comfort, yet it also felt odd, saying goodbye just as we were growing close.

I kissed her and said I'd see her in two weeks.

Chapter 14

LATE THE NEXT morning, I came down to find Dad and Gladys at the kitchen table in bathrobes eating cantaloupe and cottage cheese. They offered me the last slice, but I declined.

"You sure?" Gladys said, rising from the table. "It'll just get thrown away." I nodded and, with a shrug, Gladys carried the plate to the garbage, scraped away the cantaloupe, and left to get changed.

My father cleared the remaining dishes, his shoulders sloped over the low sink as he washed them.

"Lonnie's in town," I said.

He reached a plate to the dish rack, grimacing slightly. "Oh yeah?" He took up a fork and sponged it. "She okay?"

"Sure," I said. "Why wouldn't she be?"

"Good," he said, taking up a plate.

Gladys returned in a flowered sarong slit to the waist, a red bathing suit underneath.

"What do you think?" Gladys said to me, spinning around.

"Looks good," I said, wondering if she even remembered the fight over the watch.

"Harry?"

"Beautiful," he said, glancing over from the sink.

"She's got a new boyfriend," I said to my father.

"Who does?" Gladys said, and my father told her Lonnie was back. "What for this time?" Gladys said. "Where is she staying?"

I told her Lazy Point and she nodded. "Probably a good place for her."

"With the poor people?" I said.

"She may think poorly of herself," Gladys said, "but Lonnie isn't poor."

From the window I watched them walk out to the car, my father hunching forward.

They weren't gone five minutes when the Mustang rumbled up the driveway. Lewis climbed out, Lonnie sliding after him through his door.

"Hey bro," she said, moving past me to the refrigerator.

"Lonnie," I said, "they're going to notice."

"They owe me."

"But taking so much—"

"You can't take what's yours," she said, leaning down, opening the crisper. "If you don't understand that, stay away from me."

"Why not talk to him?"

Lonnie straightened up and glared at me. "That man tried to kill me."

"Come on, Lonnie."

She turned back to the refrigerator. "Spend some time in jail, little boy. You'd be surprised what you realize."

"I'm just saying—"

"Ricky," she said, spinning back, "I got beaten up and they put me in jail. Me, the victim."

"On what charge?"

"This guy tries to fucking kill me, and they lock *me* up, bleeding, two broken ribs . . ."

"They had to have a reason."

"Oh they had a reason," she said, again filling bag. "They always have a reason."

"How does Dad fit in?"

Lonnie folded the bag closed, sighed, and straightened. "Shit like that doesn't just happen. You don't just suddenly find yourself walking the streets." She peered at me with dark eyes. "You've got to be locked out first."

"Why not talk to him?" I said.

"Stop it!" Lonnie held her hands a few inches from each ear, as if corralling a pain larger than her head. "You don't see it?" she said. "You don't see the way he lives, the *weight* on that man?"

Lonnie finished filling the bag with food, then went to the liquor cabinet and took a bottle of bourbon and a bottle of ginger ale. She looked around the room a last time, peering out from somewhere inside herself, and walked toward the door.

"Lonnie," I said, wanting to ask her to try one more time. But I realized there was no use. "We'll come visit you in Lazy Point," I said.

The Saturday that Joany was due to return, I didn't hear from her, so the next morning I biked out to Freetown,

Jackie sending me upstairs where I found Joany lying on her bed in headphones.

Joany gazed at me, unsurprised, and I sat beside her and removed the headphones.

"What's wrong?" I said.

She shook her head.

"Joany," I said.

She turned to the window. "You don't need to know," she said.

"I *want* to know."

"Just let me listen to my song," she said, putting the headphones back on.

I removed them a second time. "Joany," I said, "what's going on?"

I sat there waiting until finally she blew out a long breath, still looking out the window. "We sleep together one time," she said, "one single time."

"What are you talking about?"

She turned and glared at me. "You really want to know?"

"Yes."

"I'm pregnant."

"*What?*"

"You heard me," she said.

I stood and walked across the room, feeling an odd mix of pride and disbelief. "How do you know?"

"I missed my period over a week ago, which I *never* do, and yesterday and today I took tests. Both were positive."

"You sure it's by me?" I said stupidly.

"*Ricky.*"

"Didn't you use birth control?"

"Didn't you?" Joany said.

"Apparently not," I said.

I returned to the bed and sat beside her.

"So now that you know, what do you want to do?" she said.

"What do you mean?"

"Ricky, I'm *pregnant.* What do you want to do?"

But the question didn't make sense to me because I couldn't conceive of any options. "You mean *when?*" I said.

"When *what?*" Joany said.

I was only aware of one option, yet I couldn't say the word. "When you want to do it."

"Goddammit, Ricky. Say what you want to do."

"End the pregnancy," I said.

"You mean have an abortion?"

"Yes," I said.

The next day I found Joany in the same place. She smiled at me as I entered but it was an underwater smile, bleary, distant. She told me her aunt had given her the name of a doctor in New York and she had an appointment in four days, the Thursday before Labor Day weekend.

"I don't expect you to come," she said.

"Of course I'm coming. I'm as responsible as you are."

"So you'll let them stick a tube up you and suck out a baby?"

"No Joany. But I'll go with you. And I'll pay for it."

"What a gentleman," she said.

"Stop it."

"Dammit, Ricky. There's a baby growing inside me."

"Are you saying you want to keep it?"

"My body wants to keep it."

"Joany, you're sixteen years old, you *can't*."

"Of course I can't! It's just not so simple."

"Okay," I said, "okay." I sat beside her. "Just tell me what you need me to do."

Joany blinked slowly, growing tired.

"How about we go see a movie?" I said. "Take your mind off it."

"My stomach's upset," she said. "I'm staying home."

Each of the next three days I called in the morning, then again in the afternoon before going to work, but Joany felt sick so I didn't see her until the day we went to New York. I dipped into my savings for the five hundred dollars, and we met at the East Hampton train station.

We boarded the train, and Joany sat by a window, turning her body to gaze out at the passing potato fields, neither of us speaking as we entered the suburbs, then the row houses of Jamaica where we switched trains.

"You never told me what happened with those art schools," I said, Joany again at the window gazing out.

"Nothing happened," she said. "I visited."

"Are you going?"

"We can't afford it."

"But what about us?" I asked. "I've already got my ticket to Rhode Island."

Joany turned from the window and faced me. "How can you ask that now?"

"I'm leaving in six days."

"Ricky, we're on our way to have an abortion. How can you ask about us?"

"Then when can I? If not now, when?"

"You don't understand, do you?" she said.

"Understand *what*?"

Joany shook her head and looked back out the window.

As we walked the ten blocks from the train station to the clinic it began to drizzle, and at the clinic's entrance a man in a yellow slicker stepped out of an adjacent doorway with a placard that held an enlarged photograph of a fetus in a dumpster, below it in bold red letters, PLEASE DON'T KILL YOUR BABY. I pulled Joany in with one arm, forearmed the guy aside with the other, and we entered the building.

After filling out the forms, Joany came and sat beside me on a couch, opposite a weary looking woman and two weary children. To the side sat a young couple speaking in whispers. Joany slid close beside me.

A nurse came out and called Joany's name, and Joany turned to me with fear in her eyes.

"I don't know if I can," she said.

I didn't know what to say—encourage her, implore her, hatch an alternate plan, propose we get engaged, have the kid and see what the hell happens?

Joany watched me another moment, then rose to her feet and followed the nurse through the swinging door.

Chapter 15

I SLID THE LAST rack of dishes into the machine and strolled out of the kitchen to where Lance, Battle, and Higgins were hanging in the alcove, Henclik and Ben sitting at the bar.

"Let's get a beer," Lance said, the two of us stepping over to order. "She told me what happened," he said.

"What'd she say?"

"*What happened.* How many versions of it are there?"

"You mean New York and all that?"

"Yes, Ricky. The pregnancy, the abortion." Lance ordered beers and we each placed a five on the bar. "What," he said, "you didn't want her to tell me?"

"Not really, no."

"I'm the girl's brother."

"It's just," I began, but didn't know what it was. "Guess it makes me look stupid."

"Her fault as much as yours." He took a pull of beer. "Just don't make the same mistake again."

"I doubt we'll have to worry about that."

"Anyway," Lance said, "you ain't the only sorry soul in here." He motioned toward Higgins and Battle leaning against the wall. "Hey, losers," he called, "get over here for a beer." Then he called to Henclik and Ben a few stools down. Henclik joined us but Ben stayed put.

"What's his problem?" Higgins said.

"You know Ben," Henclik said.

"I don't." Higgins looked at Lance. "You know Ben?"

"Nope," Lance said.

"Everybody cool," Higgins said, "till he walk in and start muggin that sour face."

"Fuck him," Battle said, holding up his beer. "To the team."

"Nah man," Higgins said. "Everybody else cool."

"Chill," Lance said.

"I'm chill," Higgins said, and walked over to Ben, sidled up beside him, and ordered from the bartender. A beer came and he slid it in front of Ben, who, staring straight ahead, slid it back. Higgins strolled back to us and handed the beer to Henclik, who now had two.

"See him dis me?" Higgins said.

"Let him be," Lance said. "Boy's got enough problems."

"Somebody offer you something, you take it," Higgins said.

"He's just a dumb-ass bubby," Henclik said, "doesn't know any better."

"He knows better," Higgins said, and walked back to Ben, the rest of us following.

"What's up with you, man?" Higgins said. But Ben didn't answer.

"Come on, Ben," Henclik said.

Ben looked at him. "Whose side you on?"

Henclik held up both hands up and backed away.

"Whose side *you* on?" Higgins said.

"My side," Ben said.

"You against the world."

Ben turned his whole body and glared at Higgins with bloodshot eyes. "You ain't the world."

"So what you gonna do?" Higgins said, sliding closer, nearly touching elbows on the bar.

Ben looked at him. "Used to be Freetown stayed in Freetown."

"Come on fellas," I said, leaning between them, "you should hear yourselves."

"Me?" Higgins said, "I should hear myself? Listen," he said to Ben, "you been getting uglier and uglier all year. So whatever it is, Ricky stepping in and taking your run, or cause your girl—"

Before Higgins could finish, Ben jumped off the stool and pressed a fist against Higgins' chest. "My problem is you," he said.

"You're seeing this," Higgins said to Lance. Then back to Ben, "So let's go."

Ben turned and marched to the door with Higgins behind him, the rest of us following.

When he reached the sidewalk, Ben turned and faced Higgins and they lunged straight into each other. A crowd gathered and the bouncers looked on from the door—the fight was off Dog House property—Higgins freeing himself from Ben's grasp, bouncing in place, and firing a flurry of punches, Ben moving in against the barrage, clutching Higgins around the waist and dragging him to the ground. On his back, Higgins continued throwing short punches at Ben's head, Ben pinning his shoulder against Higgins' chest and working himself to his knees, reaching blindly for Higgins' face, planting the heel of a hand against Higgins' nose, stacking one hand atop the other and raising himself onto his arms. Higgins cried out as blood gushed beneath Ben's hands, and Lance stepped over, grabbing Ben from behind and dragging him off.

Higgins jumped up, wild-eyed, the blood on his face glossy in the light from the street, and Lance waited till Ben was still, then released him.

"We ain't done," Higgins said, glaring across at Ben.

Ben stepped toward him. "You want more?"

Higgins stepped forward, positioning himself to throw a punch but instead swung a foot, the blow landing with a thump to Ben's side, keeling him over, Higgins firing a volley of punches at Ben's head, dropping him to his knees, Ben working his way back to his feet, as if against a strong wind, one eye nearly swollen closed.

"All year," Ben said, Higgins pausing, breathing heavily. "I gotta listen to Freetown running its mouth."

"Ben," Lance warned.

"I'm gonna tear out that fucking tongue," Ben said, and he stepped forward, Higgins taking a step back and unleashing a right to Ben's jaw, following with another kick to the ribs.

Ben fell to his knees and Higgins kicked again, hitting the same spot, dropping Ben onto his side where he rolled into a ball, pulling his knees up over crossed arms.

"I'm running my mouth now!" Higgins screamed down at him, pumping heavy breaths, pacing a few steps one way, then back.

Ben got himself up to one knee and looked over at us, his swollen face catching the light. Higgins' pacing slowed, and he turned toward Lance and Battle who each grabbed an arm.

I knelt beside Ben and one of the bouncers handed me a small towel, behind him Higgins, Lance, and Battle moving off down the sidewalk.

I watched them walk out from under the streetlight, waiting for Lance to turn back, but he never did, and they kept on until their dark figures had melted into the night.

Chapter 16

T HE DAY AFTER the fight, I stayed in bed until mid-afternoon, then wandered down to the beach for a dip, the day hot and muggy, returning to find a note on my dresser from Tessy saying to come to dinner at Lonnie's house on Lazy Point.

Biking over the Cranberry Hole Bridge, the day cooling but the bay side still hot, I settled into a slow cruise through the patch of oak woods into the open marsh, reaching Lazy Point and seeing the Mustang in a parking spot worn through the beach grass a few houses before the Brister's.

After the fight, I'd driven Ben home in his truck, stashing my bike in the back, then rode home as the first wisps of dawn lightened the eastern sky.

Like the other small houses on the point, Lonnie's sat high on stilts, the vertical siding a dull pink worn away in spots to a weathered gray. I climbed the flight of creaking stairs and found Lewis on the narrow wrap-around deck, shirtless in jeans, smoking a cigarette.

"The little brother," he said.

"Lonnie home?" I said.

Lewis motioned with his chin toward the house just as Lonnie stepped through the door. She reached over and pinched Lewis' cheek.

"Don't I pick the cutest men?" she said.

Lonnie led me around the deck to the backside where it widened from a walkway to a full deck overlooking the marsh. Her easel stood in a corner with the start of a painting—the radio tower that sat a half mile or so away rising up like a dark skeleton before a slate gray backdrop that could have been the ocean, sky, or both.

"Like it?" she asked, and I looked again to see if I'd missed something. "That's just the beginning," she said. "Couple osprey, a little color, and who knows."

"She's been saying that for a month." Tessy stood in the doorway.

"Yeah, well," Lonnie said, "the light is finally changing. Everything gets flattened out in summer."

"I love autumn," Tessy said.

"When all the creeps go back where they came from," Lonnie said, pointing across the marsh.

Beyond the radio tower, standing in the slimmest stretch of land between Amagansett and Montauk, ocean and bay a few hundred yards apart, we could see the unbroken line of traffic on Montauk highway.

"They're like insects," Lonnie said.

After eating, the four of us sat on the narrow front deck with beers, Gardiner's Bay before us, Napeague Harbor to the side, above it the descending sun.

The sound of a motor interrupted the silence and Wesley's pickup rumbled past, his arm hanging out the window, head back against the seat.

"Wesley!" I called.

The truck eased to a stop, and I descended the stairs and jogged over, giving Guts a pat.

"How's Ben?" I asked.

"He'll live," Wesley said. "Said you brung him home."

"I couldn't stop the fight, Wes. It was like—"

He raised his hand. "If he hadn't a run into that kid, he'd a run into something worse."

I pointed back to the house. "My sister just moved here," I said.

"Danny Griffith's place," he said, gazing up at the house. "They moved to North Carolina. I'm glad it's rented to locals."

"I'm leaving Tuesday," I said.

"College?" he said. "We may not be here when you come back."

"North Carolina?"

"Won't happen till it happens, bub. But between you and me and a few Indian ghosts, we're thinking about it."

"Well," I said, "if I don't see you. . . "

Wesley nodded, squinting at me. "Tell your sister if she needs anything, come give a knock."

He fluttered the hand dangling from the window and drove off.

Back on the deck, the four of us sat side by side, the sun burning down to a deep orange as it dropped toward the strip of land across the harbor, the first evening crickets beginning to call.

"So when's Joe College leaving?" Lonnie said.

"Four days," I said.

"Lance going too?"

"Says he is," I said, and noticed Tessy sulking. "What's wrong?" I said.

Tessy stared at her hands, squeezing them open and closed. "How am I supposed to keep living there?" she said.

"Don't," Lonnie said. "Stay here."

"Where will I sleep?"

"On the couch," Lonnie said.

Tessy turned to me, her eyes filling with the fear of what had happened in Florida.

Lewis, at the end of our row of chairs, leaned forward, braced himself, and stood up, the sun just touching land.

"I get the Lazy, but I don't get the Point," he said, larynx bobbing in his throat, and headed inside.

"I can't," Tessy said to Lonnie. "Not again."

"Suit yourself," Lonnie said.

Tessy gasped lightly and gripped the arms of her chair, and Lonnie went in for another round, returning with a beer for me, a glass of bourbon for herself.

She held her glass out to Tessy. "Drink some of this."

Tessy shook her head, staring at the smoldering sky the sun had left behind.

"It's not like I have a choice," I said to Lonnie.

"Stop it," Lonnie said. "Please. Or she'll just go on." Lifting her drink, she gestured toward the darkening bay and drew in a deep breath. "It's like those guys in the civil war who got their legs cut off without anesthesia. Hurts like hell for a while, but you manage."

"Thanks a lot," Tessy said.

"Don't mention it," Lonnie said, tipping her glass, taking a swallow.

The three of us sat quietly as the night closed in from the east, Tessy slinking lower in her chair, Lonnie staring off at what was now a slim ribbon of fire along the western horizon.

"Lon?" I said.

She shook her head and sighed.

"You okay?" I said.

"I'm just tired," she said. "Dog tired."

I slid my chair over and squeezed her arm and she looked at me, offered a half-hearted smile, and turned back to the disappearing day.

Coming up the drive, I saw my father's figure through the window to his study, walked in the house, and knocked on his door. I heard a drawer slide open and closed, he said "Come in," and I sat in the empty chair before his desk, my father peering at me over reading glasses.

"Get off work early?" he asked.

"Yeah," I said, not bothering to tell him I'd had the night off.

"Got enough money saved?"

"What're you working on?" I asked.

"A business deal with Gladys' brother, Corky. We're investing in a restaurant."

"I'll be the dishwasher," I said. "I'll make it my career."

"It's still a ways off," he said, looking back at his papers.

"I was kidding," I said, looking around the small room, at the shelf of books and at Gladys' desk butted against his. "You must think I'm an idiot."

He removed his glasses and looked at me. "What's this?"

"You think I'm an idiot."

"An underachiever perhaps, not an idiot."

"Is that a 'Yes'?"

He tried to stare me down, but I was too tired to look away.

"This conversation doesn't seem to be going anywhere," he said, putting his glasses back on and returning to his papers.

"Every time I talk to you," I said, "it's like there's some right thing to say and I never seem to say it. Never even come close."

"That's nonsense."

"See?"

"I'm not buying it, Ricky. If you want to play the victim, find somebody else to persecute you."

"Then tell me what I should be saying. When I walk into your study, what should I say?"

He again removed his glasses. "First of all, you don't badger the person you're supposed to be visiting. That would be a good start. Second, if you don't have something specific to say, it's probably not a good idea in the first place."

"Then I'll try again." I stood up and walked out.

"Hey Dad," I said, reentering.

He blinked slowly, growing frustrated.

"I want to ask you about Lonnie." I hesitated, then continued. "I want to know if you ever tried to hurt her."

"What's your problem, Ricky?"

"She thinks you did," I said.

"Ricky," he said, "you're badgering me. You want to know what to say when you walk into my study? Try, 'Hey Pop, anything I can do to help out around here?' Try that."

"But I honestly want to know. Lonnie comes home from Florida and won't even speak with you. She's got this convict boyfriend, this beat-up car . . . "

"That's her business."

"Not when she's over here stealing food. Even if she's not stealing food, she's my sister. But when I try to talk to her, the second I mention your name, she loses it."

My father inhaled deeply, stretching tight the tendons in his neck. "I am not responsible for Lonnie's emotions, nor for yours, nor anybody else's."

"How about yours?"

"Ricky."

"I'm just asking."

"You're not asking anything, you're insinuating. You're blaming."

"I'm asking you how you feel about your daughter."

He took another deep breath and sighed. "You said I wasn't responsible for my emotions."

"Doesn't it bother you that we can't talk, that we can't even sit in the same room without—" I hesitated, searching for the word— *"resentment?"*

"Speak for yourself."

"If you'll speak for yours."

"Ricky, I'm warning you."

"Why can't we talk about you?"

His voice strained beneath the effort to control it. "Because you're badgering," he said.

I held out opened hands. "Maybe I am," I said. "But I just want to know how you feel."

"That does not give you the right to come in here and attack me."

"Dad, I'm only asking—"

"Yes, attack me!" His face flushed with blood. "I'm tired of walking around this house, *my* house, like I'm on trial. I'm tired of walking around a bunch of spoiled kids who think I owe them something."

"We only feel that way because you turned your back on us, all of us, even Mom."

He raised a finger. "Do not tell me what I've done."

"Then *you* tell me."

"No."

"Why not?"

"Because I can't!" He peered straight at me over his glasses, his eyes hard and fixed like two small black shields.

"Maybe if we got the girls," I said, "and we all—" but he held up a hand, stopping me.

He spun around in his chair and lifted a small crystal bottle filled with bourbon and a glass from the shelf, poured out half a glass, and took a swallow.

"Listen to me," he said, spinning back, "because this is all you're getting." He shifted his gaze to the window, toward the darkness. "Your mother's biggest fear was that we'd be better off without her." He took another swallow of his drink and glanced at me. "By the time she started dying she'd become convinced. 'It's better this way,' she would say."

"That's what she told Tessy," I said.

"She was always threatened by her," he said.

"Tessy?"

"Lonnie. From the time she was a little girl, Lonnie was very tough, very demanding, and your mother couldn't handle her. To the point where if she saw Lonnie and me together she felt threatened. Your mother was extremely sensitive."

"Sounds paranoid," I said.

He blinked slowly. "Very early on," he said, "I had to make a conscious decision to put your mother first. A man who doesn't put the woman first is asking for trouble."

"Even if it means abandoning his child," I said.

"The woman has to come first," he said.

"And now it's Gladys," I said.

"Now it's Gladys."

"No wonder Lonnie is so mad," I said. "She's been abandoned not once but twice."

"Ricky."

"But why marry again so quickly?"

He sucked a breath in through his nose. "After losing your mother, I didn't know where to turn."

"Why not to us?" But as soon as I asked the question, I knew the answer: How could he have turned to us, especially Lonnie, whom he'd already forsaken? "Dad," I said, "Lonnie would have forgiven you if you'd asked her. I bet she still would."

"It was too much," he said, shaking his head. "I needed a fresh start."

My father turned from me and peered out the window into the darkness as if the light of the study, and I, were too much to bear.

I quietly rose and left.

Chapter 17

TRAIN TICKETS WERE twenty-five percent off with three days advanced purchase, so two days after the fight, I called Lance to see if he wanted to save a few bucks. Getting no answer, I went to the train station and bought my ticket.

Back at the house, Gladys met me at the door and asked if I was busy tomorrow. "We'd like to have a little farewell barbecue," she said.

"A barbecue?" I said.

"To wish you well," she said. "I called Lonnie and Tessy. Can you make it around five?"

"I'll check with the Dog House, see if I can go in late. You said Lonnie's coming?"

"I only spoke with Tessy. She said she'd tell Lonnie."

I went to the phone and dialed their house. Tessy said Lonnie wasn't coming, and when Tessy put her on, Lonnie told me it was out of the question.

"Just stop in and say goodbye," I said.

"Goodbyes are maudlin," Lonnie said.

"There'll be food," I said, but Lonnie didn't answer. "Come on, Lon. Stop by for a quick bite, then take off."

Lonnie was silent a minute before speaking. "Okay," she said, "but only to say goodbye. To *you*. Then I'm leaving."

The next afternoon, I returned from the ocean to find Gladys in the kitchen shaping hamburger patties, my father reclining on the back deck with a drink, taking stock of the shrubbery, the maples and privet surrounding the yard having grown tall and lush.

"This is a place," he said, his voice dreamy, disconnected, as I sat beside him, "you'll always want to come back to."

At first I thought he meant our home, which sounded odd, but then I realized he meant the East End. "They're trying to ruin it alright," he said, "tourists, locals, everybody. But we'll keep fighting."

He took a sip of his drink. "The first time we drove out here I knew this was where we had to be."

"When was that?" I asked.

"Only Lonnie was born then, and your mother—" he paused, glancing toward the kitchen— "she couldn't stand the suburbs. Felt trapped. Then we drove out here and saw this place. Didn't have a penny of savings—I was teaching then—but once we heard the price, well, I knew we'd find a way." My father lifted his eyes, squinting at the blue sky above the privet.

"Your mother called this *Shangri La*," he said. "The place was a shambles, but she was never happier."

"If I was coming from somewhere else," I said, "maybe I'd see it that way too."

Gladys, changed into a lime sarong and matching hoop earrings, joined us on the deck and the three of us waited for Lonnie and Tessy, Gladys telling me about the Sentinels' latest success, pushing through the rezoning ordinance for all areas over aquifer, including Lazy Point.

"If we let them," she said, meaning the locals, including the group that had opposed them, the Bonac Baymen, which included the haul-seiners, "these people would build on eighth-acre plots."

"Of all people," my father said, "you'd think the fishermen would want to preserve the quality of life out here."

"What about their families?" I said. "Isn't that part of 'quality of life'?"

"Sure it is," my father said, the squint of his eyes tightening as he again shifted his gaze to the sky. "But not the small family, the *big* family."

I was just about to give up on Tessy and Lonnie and go back to the beach when Tessy came through the screen door in her white dress, now more gray than white.

"Oh," Gladys said, surprised.

Next, Lonnie came through the door, wearing tight jeans, high-top sneakers, and the same hoop earrings as Gladys, only Lonnie's were red.

My father said hello with a smile and offered Lonnie a drink, something I'd never seen him do, and Lonnie, avoiding his eyes, said in a humdrum voice she'd take a Rob Roy.

The sun descended past the peak of the house, and we sat on the deck in the shade, my father and Gladys in chaise lounges, the rest of us on cushioned chairs, Lonnie sitting stiffly on the edge of hers. Tessy and I sipped iced tea, the rest cocktails.

"So," Gladys said, "we're all together."

"Yeah, to say good-bye," Tessy said glumly.

"You're leaving this weekend, right?" Gladys said to me.

"Tuesday," I said. "Day after Labor Day."

"You didn't know when he was leaving?" Lonnie said to Gladys.

"Old Ricky," my father said, "doesn't offer up a lot of information."

"No wonder," Lonnie said.

"Anyway," Gladys said, "here's to a great year," and she lifted her glass, the rest of us following suit.

Lonnie swallowed the last of her drink and without looking at my father said she'd take another, Gladys swallowing the last of hers and saying she'd take one too, and my father went in with their empty glasses.

"Hard to believe," Gladys said, looking appreciatively out at the yard, "another summer's almost over."

"You sound like you've lived here all your life," Lonnie said.

"Sometimes it feels like I have," Gladys said.

"Did it ever occur to you," Lonnie said, "that before you there was a complete family living here?"

"She means," I said quickly, "everything changed kind of fast."

"She knows what I mean," Lonnie said.

"Yes," Gladys said, "that you're not ready to accept me."

"Exactly," Lonnie said.

"All we wanted," Tessy said, "was time to work things through."

"I'm sorry," Gladys said. "But sometimes things take on a life of their own."

"Yeah," Lonnie said, but my father appeared with the drinks and the conversation ceased.

The shade spread across the back yard as my father grilled hamburgers and hot dogs. Gladys brought out a plate of sliced tomato and a bowl of potato salad, and we sat at the picnic table in the yard. Tessy served herself a slice of tomato and a spoonful of potato salad.

"Not hungry?" my father said to Tessy.

"I'm vegetarian," Tessy said.

"Since when?" he said.

Lonnie dropped her fork on the plate and stopped chewing the food in her mouth.

"He just forgot," Tessy said.

Lonnie took a sip of her drink, washing down the food. "It's not okay," she said, "it's criminal. You're so busy with your Sentinels, or whatever they are, you don't even know your daughter is vegetarian. Tell me," she said, her eyes boring in on my father, "when's my birthday? When's Ricky's?"

"That's enough, Lonnie," he said.

"No." Lonnie stood up and pointed at him. "Your own children are all going to hell and you have no clue. I'm in Florida getting the shit beat out of me, thrown in jail. Tessy can hardly walk down the street she's so scared, and Mr. Basketball here is sneaking off to Manhattan for abortions."

"What are you talking about?" I said.

"The whole town knows," Lonnie spat. "Everybody except your parents."

"My god," Gladys said, looking at me, "what happened?"

"He realized," Lonnie said, shifting her eyes from Gladys to my father, "it's better to abort a baby *before* it's born than after." She stood there glaring at him but he wouldn't look back.

"I always thought you hated me," Lonnie continued, "because I interrupted your wonderful life together. But that was a lie. You had no wonderful life, you were both sick."

"Lonnie," Gladys said, standing up across the table, "we've been trying to reconstruct our lives, same as you."

"I wasn't talking about you," Lonnie said, her mouth twisting with disgust. "I was talking about him and our mother. Somebody we actually loved. Somebody he actually loved."

"That's enough," my father said, standing, three of them now up. "You will not insult Gladys."

"You do," Lonnie said, "why shouldn't I? Your life with her is one continuous insult, the way you're all bent over like she's a thousand pounds tied around your neck. He used to stand up straight," Lonnie said to Gladys.

"So did I," Gladys said, her voice tightening. "Did you ever think the weight on him might be you? It might be his own children?"

Lonnie stepped around me toward Gladys. "What the hell do you know?" she said. "You're a goddammed mistress."

"You won't bully me, Lonnie," Gladys said, stepping forward.

"Not only are you unwelcome," Lonnie said, "you're too stupid to realize it."

Gladys took another step to within a couple feet of Lonnie. "I would never call you stupid, Lonnie," she said, "but it's not me whose time is up here."

Lonnie's eyes widened with rage. "You whore," she said, and in one quick motion snapped a hand across Gladys' face.

Gladys stared back at her, for a moment seeming overmatched, but then her body stiffened, and she swung back, striking Lonnie with a crisp smack.

Stunned, Lonnie turned to my father, then to Tessy, and finally to me. But there was nothing we could do, the blow already struck, and Lonnie whirled away and ran.

Tessy and I followed, but by the time we reached the edge of the driveway Lonnie was already speeding away, a hail of gravel raining down behind her.

Chapter 18

THE DAY BEFORE Labor Day, Sunday, I biked to the Williams', turning onto Three Mile Harbor Road into a brisk northern wind. A cold front had come through overnight and, just like that, it felt like autumn, the trees rustling loudly, as if in protest of the coming cold.

I found Lance sitting on the steps outside the kitchen, a brown bottle of beer dangling from his fingers. I hadn't seen him since the fight three nights earlier.

"If it isn't Cool Motion," he said, shoulders slumped, clothes looking slept in.

"I'm glad you're here," I said, leaning my bike against the house. "How's Higgins?"

"He's okay," Lance said, "how's your boy?"

"My boy?"

"How's Ben?"

"What's this 'my boy'?"

"Forget it. Beer?"

"Ben was hurt bad, Lance, so I took him home."

"And Higgins is in the hospital."

"His nose?"

Lance smiled and shook his head. "Yeah, Cool, his nose. Your boy Ben fucked him up so bad he's lying in Southampton Hospital wishing he'd never seen him."

"What are you saying?"

"Higgins' big brother—you know Teddy right, big dude, played football at Pitt?" He stared at me, waiting for a response, his eyes so bloodshot they seemed ready to bleed. "Seems Teddy found out about the fight before Higgins got home. Somebody called him with a report, not just incriminating Higgins, but Freetown too. White people like that, Cool? Y'all rat each other out?"

"As a matter of fact, yes," I said.

"Nah," Lance said, shaking his head, "it's different. Cause we're afraid. You hear me?" He shook his head. "We're always watching for somebody to fuck up, and soon's he does, we run to that phone, call his kin to report they ain't nothin but lowly negroes after all."

Lance took a swallow of beer and I kicked at loose rocks on the driveway, thinking maybe he was right, maybe it was different.

"So check it out, Cool. When Higgins walked in after the fight, Teddy was waiting for him. With a—guess what?"

I shrugged.

"Guess."

"A knife."

"Teddy's a football hero, solid citizen, it ain't no knife."

"A bat," I said.

"Nah, but that's a good guess, Cool. But nah, when Higgins walked in the door, Teddy took him out with a two-by-four." Lance pursed his lips, gripping an imaginary board and swinging it across his body. "*Uunngh*. Like that. Split his head wide open. Two hundred stitches."

"He okay?"

"His nose is okay, Cool."

"Stop fuckin' with me, Lance. I've been dealing with some shit too."

"That why you come out here to Freetown, get away from that shit? You want to run some ball, Ricky? Let's go get Higgins, you tight with him too, right?" He peered up at me, challenge in his red eyes. "Cause two hours a day you run on the same court, you tight with him."

"So I'm not Higgins' friend," I said, "is that it? Not your friend? Go ahead and say it."

"You say it."

The way he sneered up at me, I was tempted. "And you definitely don't think I could be Joany's friend," I said.

"I don't know," Lance said, staring me in the eye, "could you?"

I didn't answer, and Lance stood up and walked a few paces, then turned back.

"Higgins is in a coma, Ricky."

"*What*? And you don't tell me?"

"You just said you had your own problems."

I stared back at his bleeding eyes, again thinking maybe he was right, what good could I do out here? But looking at Lance, I wondered how much he could do, how much anybody could.

"You should have told me," I said.

"Nah, man," Lance said. "You came out here to run some ball, maybe get some trim."

"Lance, if this is about Joany . . ."

"Aw, you're my best friend, Cool."

"I kept telling myself," I said, looking from Lance into the woods across the street, "let him be. He's got a lot on his mind, he'll come around." I stepped over to him. "I know you're not going to Bryant," I said. "I already bought my ticket. But you keep acting like there's all this *real shit* going on."

Lance looked at me a minute, then bent and snatched a handful of grass, sat back on the stoop, separating the blades of grass on his palm.

"Yeah, I'm staying," he said.

"Is it Tanya?"

"It's a lot of shit," he said. "You hear me? It's Tanya, it's Tanya's father, it's cancer, it's Higgins, whose own family won't even go to the hospital. Who do you think sat with him the last two nights in Intensive Care? It's this place—" he threw his hand toward the house— "Jackie working and my little brother *deserving* to have somebody here. It's East Hampton, it's Freetown . . . But you always want one simple reason."

"Lance," I said, "how am I supposed to know if you don't tell me?"

"Goddammit, Ricky." Lance stood up, peering at me with his red eyes. "I *am* telling you," he said. "I *been* telling you." Tears streamed down his face. "You want shit spelled out . . ." He broke off, looking at me, water overflowing his red eyes.

"I hear you," I said, but he kept peering at me like he couldn't see me, like I'd disappeared beneath a sea of other worries. "Lance," I said, "I hear you."

"His own brother," he said finally, and he blinked so slowly his eyes barely reopened.

I put an arm around him, helped him back to the stoop, and Lance sat limply beside me, the two of us gazing down the street into the dark tunnel of trees that led further into Freetown.

Before leaving the Williams', I went inside and checked Joany's room but found it empty. Biking home, I decided to head out to Lazy Point, hanging a left before the train tracks, curved through the woods, a patch of sand dunes, and into the open marsh.

Tessy answered the door. The temperature having dropped into the sixties, she wore a loose sweatshirt over the white dress. I asked how Lonnie was doing and she shook her head.

"They drank and fought for two days nonstop," she said. "Then Lewis left. Took a taxi to the train station. Ricky, she's impossible."

We heard footsteps and Lonnie entered the living room carrying a suitcase, hair disheveled.

"Little Boy Wonder," she said.

"Hey, Lon," I said.

"What's our little Hamptons cruiser up to today?"

"I was wondering if you'd come by the house and talk things out with Dad and Gladys."

Lonnie caught me in a heavy unblinking gaze. "Fuck you," she said.

She set the suitcase by the door and walked groggily into the kitchen, where she pulled the freezer door open, letting it swing into the wall.

"Ricky," Tessy said, "she doesn't mean it."

"Fuck you too, Tessy," Lonnie called. "Fuck you both."

We stood there in silence listening to cracking ice cubes and clinking glass.

"You incestuous brats," Lonnie said, returning to the living room, rocking to the side, the bourbon in her glass tipping but not spilling. "Tell me," she said, "how often do you two fuck?"

"Stop it, Lonnie," I said.

"Lonnie," Tessy said, "Ricky's leaving tomorrow."

"Oh my God," Lonnie said, "our little lover slash brother is leaving. What are you going to do? I know. Start fucking Lewis."

Tessy turned to me, sickened, and left the room.

"Come on, Lon," I said, guiding her to a chair.

For a moment, Lonnie sat still, gazing out the window, but when I reached over to take her drink, she jerked her arm back, spraying the liquid in an arc across the wall.

She stood up and wobbled into the kitchen.

"If you pour another, I'm leaving," I said, following her.

She swung back, gripping the bottle by its neck. "If I pour two, will you kill yourself?"

"What the hell has gotten into you?" I said.

"You two have no fucking idea about anything. You live in bubbles," she said, "fucking bubbles." She shook her head as she poured the drink. "Fucking pathetic," she said, her body wobbling but the stream of bourbon staying straight and steady.

"Okay," I said, "I'm out of here."

Lonnie turned and glared at me. "Is that a threat?"

"No," I said.

"Don't threaten me with your petty sentimental bullshit. All your fucking going away, and your missing each other, and your bullshit clingy desperate excuses. Leave me the fuck out of it." She glared another moment, then blinked and took a long breath. "Now if you'll go hop on your scooter," she said, "I've got more packing to do."

"It's a bike," I said. "Where you going?"

"As soon as my low-life boyfriend gets back, I'm going to Florida." She turned away and walked toward her bedroom door, her path off by a full two feet, at the last second stumbling at an angle through the doorway, grabbing the doorknob as she passed, pulling it closed behind her.

Tessy re-emerged and said in a whisper that Lewis had called that morning to have his mail forwarded.

"He's already there," she said. "He's not coming back."

Chapter 19

Labor Day night, after my last shift of summer, I came out of the kitchen and found Henclik leaning against the wall, cool September air streaming through the near-empty bar from the open front door to the rear doors to the deck.

Henclik looked me over, from my loosely laced high-tops to my food-splattered sweatshirt.

"Heard from Ben?" I asked.

"He's back home, fishing." Henclik swigged from his beer. "Any word on Higgins?"

"No, but Lance should be here soon."

Henclik tilted his empty beer at me, and when I nodded, he pivoted and moseyed toward the bar, the place oddly quiet, only a smattering of people, mostly locals, while outside on Montauk Highway a steady stream of loaded-down cars headed back to wherever they'd come from.

Henclik handed me a green bottle of beer.

"You heard Lance isn't going to Bryant?" I said.

"Cause of Higgins?"

"Lot of reasons," I said. "Family, girlfriend . . . "

"Shit," Henclik muttered, "if I had his talent."

"Yeah," I said, taking a swallow of icy beer. "When you heading out?"

"Tomorrow."

"Me too."

Lance walked through the front door, strolled down the length of the bar and, reaching us in the back, looked me in the eye, his own eyes red and tired.

"Higgins woke up," he said, mouth spreading into a smile.

We leaned close and high-fived with both hands over our heads, and he turned and high-fived Henclik.

"Last night, right while I'm sitting there," Lance said, "he opens his eyes and looks at me. 'I can't fucking sleep,' he says. After three full days in a coma. So they kept him over night to check him out and today I went and picked him up. One minute he's near dead, next minute he's walking out the door. Took him to my house."

"I'm buying a round," Henclik said, and shuffled off to the bar.

"So what's up with you?" Lance said.

"Lonnie and my step-mom had it out," I said. "Now Lonnie's on a three-day drunk."

"Maybe it's for the best," Lance said, "them finally fighting it out."

"Maybe," I said.

"That's what we're drinking to," Lance said, pulling back his flannel shirt, worn over his game jersey, revealing a half-filled pint of Jim Beam tucked in his waist. "To starting a new chapter."

Henclik returned with beers and the three of us trooped into the bathroom. The first shot of whiskey burned into my neck and shoulders and, after two pulls each, Lance dropped the empty bottle in the trash.

"Finally got me some space," Henclik said, spreading his arms in the alcove, ambling over to the juke box where two women were flipping through the songs.

Lance and I took seats at the bar. "Here's to that sorry game of yours," I said, tapping my bottle against Lance's. "I sure won't miss having to school your ass."

"Be too busy *being* schooled," he said.

"By Tanya."

"In your dreams."

"As for that sister of yours—" I stopped short and watched him.

"Go ahead, Home," he said. "What about her?"

"Nothing," I said. "I'm just going to miss her."

I guzzled what was left of my beer, looked at the two of us in the mirror behind the bar, and spoke to Lance's reflection, his dark eyes gazing back at me.

"You really staying?"

"Yes."

"Tanya want to get married?"

"There you go with your dumb-ass reasons."

"Then why?"

"Because I ain't fooling myself."

"You can do anything you want, and you stay."

"Like what?" He turned and faced me, but I kept watching his reflection.

"Anything," I said.

"Get drafted out of Division Two? That your plan, be the one dude in history to go pro out of Bryant College?"

"I sure as hell ain't staying here."

"So go."

"I'm going."

Lance finished his beer, ordered two more, and we sat quietly drinking, looking straight ahead into the mirror, at ourselves and at the meager activity behind us, Henclik at the juke box selecting songs.

"Alright, man," Lance said, sliding off his stool and emptying his pockets, dumping a handful of change and loose singles on the bar.

"Going to Tanya's?"

He nodded and started toward the door.

"I'll call you tomorrow," I said, Lance turning back, "give you one last chance to change your mind."

Lance shook his head and walked back. Draping an arm across my shoulders, he leaned so close I had to lean away to get his eyes in focus, the pupils large and black, surrounded by a delicate rim of brown.

"It ain't going to make no difference," Lance said, "but go ahead and call."

Chapter 20

I AWOKE THE DAY of my train to a voice repeating my name and found Tessy kneeling beside the bed.

"You've got to come," she said.

I sat up and looked at the alarm clock. "Train's not till eleven-thirty," I said.

"It's Lonnie," Tessy said.

As my eyes cleared, I saw the fear in Tessy's face.

"Is she okay?" I said.

"I don't know—we have to hurry."

Though Tessy didn't drive, she'd somehow gotten to Amagansett in the Mustang. When she opened the driver-side door I thought she intended to drive back, but she slid through to the passenger's seat, and I slid in behind her. Though I hardly drove, Dad and Gladys' cars off limits, I'd had my license since turning 17 the previous fall.

At the house in Lazy Point, Tessy emerged from the driver's side after me and pointed at an angle across the marsh.

"There," she said, but I only saw the radio tower.

"At the top," Tessy said.

I noticed a black spot, which I took for an osprey nest, just beneath the blinking red light.

"That's Lonnie," Tessy said.

"You sure?"

Tessy withdrew a folded piece of paper from a pocket and handed it to me.

> Tessy,
> None of this bullshit concerns you. None of it. Or Ricky either. It's mine, just mine, and that's how I want to keep it. I love you both.
> Lonnie

"The car was here," Tessy said, "so I knew she couldn't have gone far."

Tessy led me down the street past the Bristers to the inlet, and we turned along the mucky shoreline toward the tower.

"I checked the beach, then came out here and there she was," Tessy said. "I called to her but she yelled, 'Go away.' So I went and got you."

We continued through the muck until the ground hardened into dry sand and walked a few hundred yards more to the base of the tower. Erected from steel strips forming large triangles, the tower rose from a concrete slab into a tall skeletal obelisk, its peak a good two hundred-fifty feet in the air.

I could now make out Lonnie's face, a small circle of flesh framed by dark hair blowing in the wind off the ocean, which lay beyond the dunes a few hundred yards away.

"Lonnie!" I called. "Come down and talk!"

"Leave me alone," came her answer, faint and distant in the wind.

"You're scaring us!" Tessy shouted.

Not hearing any response, I grabbed hold of the first horizontal strip of steel and lifted myself onto the tower. Climbing was difficult because of the triangular formation of each section—the utility workers had ladders to attach— but I wedged my foot into the joints and stepped up.

"Ricky!" I looked down from a height of fifteen feet or so and saw Tessy pointing up. At the top, Lonnie was leaning off the tower, holding herself with one hand. I held still a moment, then lowered myself to the ground, and Lonnie sat back again on the tower.

"Maybe we should leave," Tessy said.

"But what if she does something?" I said.

"Might be better if we weren't here."

"No," I said, "you stay. I'm going for help."

"Help?" Tessy said. "From who?"

But I didn't answer, just headed back through the marsh.

Standing by the phone in their kitchen I thought first to call my father, then the police, but finally decided on Lance.

"It's me, Ricky," I said, hearing his sleepy voice.

"The answer's no," Lance said. "Have a good trip."

"My sister Lonnie's at the top of the radio tower."

"Where you calling from?" Lance said.

"Her house, Lazy Point."

"You call the police?"

"No."

"Hang on," Lance said, "I'm on my way."

Waiting for Lance, I paced from room to room, looking over the near-empty house, a pizza box and a single empty glass on the small dining room table, three packed suitcases beside the front door.

Lance pulled up before the house, Higgins in the car beside him, and I jumped in the back.

"How you feeling?" I asked Higgins.

"I'm alright," Higgins said. "It's your sister we're worried about."

I felt a surge of gratitude but knew it was too early to thank anybody.

"Drive around to the service road off the highway," I said.

We circled the marsh and pulled onto a clear Montauk Highway, grown empty of summer traffic in a single day. I leaned over the front seat and pointed up through the windshield.

"That's her," I said.

We pulled onto the service drive to the tower where we parked beside Wesley's pickup, Wesley and Jason standing alongside Tessy, all three peering up at Lonnie.

"We seen you two walking out in the marsh," Wesley said, looking from me back to the tower. "Then we seen in binoculars what you were walking toward. She spoke to anybody?"

"Just said to leave her alone."

Wesley lowered his eyes to mine. "Then why don't you?"

"Something's wrong, Wes," I said.

"She left us a note," Tessy said.

"A goodbye note," I said.

"Lonnie!" Wesley called up through cupped hands. "You got a brother and sister down here!"

The six of us listened for an answer but none came. Wesley turned to me.

"You think she got it in her to jump?" he said.

I glanced at Tessy, and we answered together, "Yes."

"Ricky," Higgins said, "how about I climb up from behind where she can't see me?"

"And do what?" Lance said.

"Grab her," Higgins said, "I don't know. Hold her till more people get there."

"If she sees anybody coming, she'll jump," I said. "I already tried."

"Ricky," Tessy said, "we should get Dad."

"What's he gonna do?" I said.

"Talk to her," Tessy said, *"apologize."*

I looked at Lance, who said, "Just tell me what you need," and asked if he'd drive Tessy back to my father's.

As I held the door for Tessy, I told her, "Just him." Tessy nodded and closed the door.

Higgins stayed behind, and the four of us stood beside Wesley's truck, as to the south the sun reached its apex, suspended above the dunes blocking the ocean, and a southerly breeze picked up, not as strong as the day before but building, sliding over the dunes and across the narrow strip of land toward Lazy Point and the bay. I looked up at Lonnie huddled in her dark clothes, small and exposed in the growing wind.

A figure walked toward us across the marsh and as it approached I saw it was Ben. His eyes avoiding Higgins, he asked what was going on. Jason pointed up and Ben tilted back gingerly, the ribs bruised but not broken, and ran his eyes up the tower.

"That's my sister," I said.

"What the hell's she doing?" he said.

"She ain't sunbathing," Wesley said.

"Why don't somebody go up and get her?"

"Because she'll jump," Higgins said. "I already offered."

Ben turned to his father. "Ain't the fire department got nothing to catch her with?"

"Not from that height," Wesley said.

We heard crunching gravel and Lance's car approached on the service drive, my father in the passenger's seat peering up through his open window at Lonnie. He unfolded himself from the car and, the grimace softening to a painful smile, introduced himself to Wesley.

"I know who you are," Wesley said, no doubt familiar with the Sentinels.

"I appreciate your coming out here today," my father said.

"These girls are my neighbors," Wesley said.

My father turned to me. "So what's going on?" he said.

"We're afraid she's going to jump," I said.

"But what's the reason?"

"There isn't one," I said, "there's a thousand," and I walked over to a different vantage point.

My father came after me. "Ricky," he said, "how'd she get up there? What did she say?"

"This morning Tessy found a note from her that said, basically, goodbye—that all the shit was hers and she wanted to keep it that way."

"Couldn't she have meant—"

"We know what she meant."

My father shook his head, peered back up at Lonnie, and walked off, continuing in a circle around the tower, pausing every few steps to look up from a different angle.

Again reaching me, separate from the others, he squinted into the wind. "When your mother was dying," he said, "I refused to believe it."

He tilted back to gaze again at Lonnie, his mouth easing open, revealing his upper molars dark with fillings.

"Each day," he said, "Lonnie would come home from school, walk straight up to me and ask if her mother had died. I would say 'No, of course not' and Lonnie would just stomp away." A weak smile pushed into his lips. "She was always so fierce about the truth."

"She still is," I said.

My father peered at me, expression unchanged, until Tessy's voice broke the silence.

"Ricky!" she called, and I looked up and saw Lonnie standing, leaning off the tower into the wind, her head a few feet to the side of the blinking red light at the tower's peak.

"She just stood up," Tessy said.

"She's not looking down here," Lance said, "but out at the ocean."

We stood in silence watching Lonnie's figure high above, standing atop the tower as if it were a great crow's nest, Lonnie on watch for the entire East End.

"What's she looking at?" Tessy said.

"Nothing," Wesley said. "Or everything. Up there she can see a hundred miles."

Again we grew silent, watching Lonnie leaning into the wind, gazing out across the ocean.

Then I heard my father's voice. "Lonnie," he said softly, his voice filled with recognition, as if he alone knew what she could see.

"Lonnie," he repeated.

Lonnie held her position, fixed as a figurehead, leaning into the strengthening wind, until finally, she pulled her eyes from the distance and looked down.

It was impossible to tell if Lonnie looked directly at my father or if she eyed the whole group, taking in who was there. But after a moment, as if satisfied with what she saw, she again straightened, raised her eyes to the sky, and jumped.

Up to that moment, I had never wanted, never needed, anything more of myself. But as I watched my sister hurtle feet first toward the earth, her body listing slightly backward, seeming to recline, my stomach clenched into spasm, as if emptying itself, trying to locate and spit up the mistake I had made, one of us had made, the single error that had led to this moment.

But there was no mistake to recall, and I could only stand there and watch Lonnie fall, growing as she descended, her face coming briefly into focus, calm and resolute, before I closed my eyes and heard her life end with a sickeningly soft thump against the earth.

As I stood staring at Lonnie's humped body lying on its side, one leg bent grotesquely forward at the knee instead of back, I heard Tessy cry out and turned to see her running into the marsh. Jason Brister took off after her, and I turned back to find my father standing still, peering at Lonnie.

After a spell, he stepped forward and knelt beside her. He gingerly reached forward, sliding one hand beneath the foot of her broken leg and the other beneath the useless knee, gently levering the leg back, so Lonnie again seemed of a single piece.

Then he stood up and, his head hanging heavily forward, ran his eyes across the group of onlookers, as if to let each of us see his face, as if to admit, yes, he was the dead girl's father, he was the one who had brought her into the world.

Chapter 21

I DELAYED MY DEPARTURE until after the funeral four days later, sleeping on the couch in Lazy Point, Tessy and I driving the Mustang each afternoon to Amagansett to walk along the ocean, the beach vacant aside from the occasional group of standing seagulls. We'd walk for miles, slowly working our way through long troughs of silence, until the tears would surge and one of us would stop, only able to turn and face the open sea.

The day of the funeral, I drove to the house in Amagansett to get dressed, not seeing Dad and Gladys, and when I returned to Lazy Point for Tessy, she came out through the kitchen door in an elegant but simple black dress, the first dark thing I'd ever seen her wear. Her hair was brushed and silky and though her eyes were pink from days of crying, her skin was smooth and clear.

"You look beautiful," I said.

She sat beside me and smiled nervously. "It's not too much?" she said.

"It's perfect," I said.

∞

Tessy and I stood in the foyer of the church greeting the thin stream of arrivals, which included the four Bristers, Higgins, Battle, and the Williams family. The last arrivals were Dad and Gladys, Gladys saying simply "I'm sorry," giving me and Tessy each a firm hug, my father at her shoulder offering a wan smile and following Gladys to the front pew.

During the service, when the grief would rise up and overflow, I'd glance at Tessy beside me. Tears streaming steadily from her eyes, she sat up straight, head high, as if somehow presiding over things, which in terms of rightful grief, I suppose she was.

We buried Lonnie in the small Amagansett cemetery on Bluff Road overlooking the ocean, on this day a hard slate-blue flecked with white caps. When the casket was lowered, Jackie Williams stepped forward and recounted a couple of anecdotes from when she and Lonnie worked together, then read a short elegy, pausing before the final phrase, which she said was one hundred percent pure Lonnie—*more passion than pounds.*

We stood for an awkward moment waiting for someone else to speak. Thinking my father might have something prepared, something from the Sentinels, I turned to find him holding his face in one hand, clutching Gladys' arm with the other.

Finally, Wesley cleared his throat and stepped forward, saying in a soft voice he was sorry for not getting to know Lonnie better, sorry his own problems and the troubles of the haul-seiners had distracted him from someone in need who lived only a few doors away.

"The Indians out here used to say everyone gets a season of fish," he said, glancing from my father to me with a pained smile, his eyes bright and blue within the weathered visage, "a chunk of time when things start breaking their way. Some of us get it this life, some not till the next." He continued to look at me, squinting now as if clinging to some slim distant prospect. "I want to believe your sister's season is coming."

Then Tessy, my father, whose head remained bowed, and I each dropped a shovelful of dirt into Lonnie's grave.

A table of crackers, cheese, and fruit juice had been set up on a small lawn beside the cemetery and on my way over I felt a tap on my shoulder and turned to find Joany.

She led me back through the cemetery to a spot on the bluff facing into the breeze off the ocean.

"I'm sorry I didn't call," Joany said. "I needed time."

I turned and faced her, filled with a thin, ethereal hope.

"It wasn't the abortion," she said. "I had doubts from the beginning."

"Why?" I said.

"Because, Ricky, from the moment I met you, you were never really there, never *here*."

"What if I stayed?" I said.

Joany didn't answer, just shook her head and peered out off the bluff.

"I could go next semester," I said. "Or next year. And in the meantime, I could stay with Tessy on Lazy Point. She's going to be alone."

Joany turned back to me. "Ricky, you can't."

"Why not?"

"Because your life isn't here," she said. "I don't know where it is, but it's not here."

I turned from her back into the wind.

"Promise me," Joany said.

I stood there staring at the distant horizon, at the narrow crease between ocean and sky.

"Ricky," Joany said, "promise you'll go."

I hesitated a final moment, then said, "Okay, I promise."

Joany released a sigh and I felt her clasp my arm—firm, solid, the grip of both her hands.

"We'd better get back," she said.

We found the rest of the Williamses waiting by the Taurus, and Joany gave me a quick hug and climbed in the back. The others entered after her, except for Lance who waited at his door.

"Okay, man," he said, extending a hand, "I want you to go up there and give 'em hell."

"And you," I said, "you give 'em hell right here."

Lance turned and opened his door, then turned back. "You know," he said, "your calling me that day and asking me to come out to Lazy Point, that meant something."

"Your coming out there meant something," I said.

Lance eyed me another moment, then threw me a final high-five and slid in behind the wheel.

Chapter 22

T
HE NEXT DAY, I climbed on the train with a single suitcase crammed with clothes and a deflated basketball, and a backpack for my other things, including a framed photograph Tessy had handed me at the station of her, Lonnie, and me standing together on the deck of the house in Lazy Point.

For a while, as the train rolled through the potato fields of Amagansett, through East Hampton, into Bridgehampton, I was overwhelmed with doubt, and at each stop had to fight back the urge to get off. But once I reached New York City and sat there amidst the strangers waiting to switch to the New England train, the fear of leaving something behind was overtaken by a swirling anticipation of what lay ahead.

There's an odd moment late in the journey—after the morning ride to New York, the hour wait for the transfer, another couple hours chugging through Connecticut—just as you reach the Rhode Island border, when the track rises up onto a harbor crossing and the broad blue Long Island Sound comes into view. Fishers Island sits there to the right, the small hump of Block Island in the distance to the left, and between them, a slim gray line, hardly more than a shadow, the place you've spent the entire day journeying from—the East End of Long Island.

Epilogue

Missoula 1996

Over the past twelve years, I've stayed in close touch with Tessy who, after Lonnie's funeral, took over the house on Lazy Point and found a job at a shelter for runaways in Montauk. Tessy has more than a superficial understanding of why kids run off, seeing their flight not as unfortunate but as necessary, not as an escape but a calling. And when they leave the shelter, she likes to say, most of them no longer run but walk.

Tessy also began spending time with Jason Brister. When after one last season hauling seine, the Bristers sold their house and moved to North Carolina, Jason stayed behind, taking up carpentry and moving in with Tessy. The latest news is that the two of them have made an offer to buy the house.

Joany, too, is working on the East End, as artist-in-residence in the middle schools, and Tessy says Joany's had exhibitions of her work in some of the East End's top galleries. The report on Lance is that he moved into Tanya's house in Springs and started a landscaping business. Tessy says he's raking it in and just recently bought a chunk of land for his own nursery.

Dad and Gladys I talk to now and then. Major holidays, we catch up on each other's news and wish each other well. Between my father and me there's a wistfulness to our exchanges, a shared sense that the gulf between us can never be overcome, but I think from both sides the wishes are genuine.

One letter of Tessy's provided a more complete picture. A few months after I left, she wrote me about a public hearing concerning a new building ordinance that had attracted the whole town, and said that afterward my father and Wesley had gone for a beer. Tessy described Gladys driving home alone as my father climbed in Wesley's pickup, and though as it turned out my father and Gladys remained close as ever, soon after the night of the hearing they resigned their post as leaders of The Sentinels.

A ten-minute drive from my apartment in Missoula, a few miles up Pattee Canyon, sits a grown-over basketball court surrounded with shrubs, out of which rise a few Rocky Mountain Maples, their autumn leaves a mix of fiery reds and yellows. October is only a couple days away, with it my thirtieth birthday and, most likely, the season's first snowfall.

The court is where I go, still, to clear my head. In fact, I only made the team at Bryant because Coach saw me one morning playing alone in the gym. When I hammered down a two-handed dunk, he stepped through the doorway from which he'd been watching, called me over, asked

where the hell I'd come from, and said I might just be the
two-guard he was looking for. Then the season started, and
I bogged down beneath the repetition, routine, beneath the
expectation, developed patellar tendinitis, "jumper's knee,"
and ended up only playing a few minutes a game.

After college, I moved west in stages, taking a job
teaching Phys Ed at a middle school in Columbus, where
I'd followed a girl I dated senior year, then moving on
to Minneapolis to give grad school a shot, and finally to
Missoula, where for the past five years I've been keeping my
footprint light, teaching part-time, coaching in a recreation
league and, for the past year, seeing a woman who seems
to get me.

From the day we met, Sloane hasn't been threatened by
my reluctance, whether to hold hands in public or go meet
her family in Bozeman. When an overture of hers fails to
get a response, she'll just lean back and give me this amused
look, as if she can see right through me.

Yet it's been a while since she's asked me to go to
Bozeman, and when last night I told her I was considering
a move further west to northern Washington, or maybe up
to British Columbia, she gave me that smirking look, only
this one icier, the look reminding me of Lance's skepticism
when I said I didn't care if I played on the high school team.

"What did you say they called you in high school,"
Sloane asked, as if sensing my thoughts. "Mr. Cool?"

"Cool Motion," I said.

Sloane shook her head. "You are *so* transparent," she
said.

"Oooh," I said, widening my eyes, fluttering an arm on either side, "You can see through me because I'm a ghost."

"See *through* you?" Sloane said. "You wish. There's a big broken heart in the way."

Today the weather is cool, the late-afternoon shade beginning to creep across the canyon. I start out shooting layups, twenty-five with the left hand, twenty-five with the right, then dribble at a jog up the court and back, beginning to sweat despite the chill, simulating breakaways, trying to get loose enough to dunk. But with each effort, I lose another inch or two of vertical and soon can barely reach the rim. I make one last attempt, not even coming close, and walk back to the truck.

As I'm opening the pickup door, a gust of warm air surges into the canyon, rustling the leaves of the Mountain Maples behind me. I turn back and watch them swell with air, shimmer, and shudder. Then the breeze passes, and the trees again stand still.

About the Author

SHELBY RAEBECK GREW up in the hamlet of Amagansett on eastern Long Island. After earning a BA at Eckerd College and graduate degrees at Boston University and the University of Utah, he taught at schools and colleges in New York City, Virginia, Maryland, Louisiana, and California, before returning in 2000 with his family to Long Island's East End. He now lives in Springs.

Much of Raebeck's writing, including *Louse Point: Stories from the East End,* the novel, *Sparrow Beach,* and the one-person play, *Fremont's Farewell,* is set on the East End.

His most recent novel, *Wonderless,* zooms out from Long Island to chronicle the cross-country trek of an ever-growing group of New York City high school dropouts, their numbers steadily growing as they blaze an indelible trail from east coast to west.

With *Amagansett '84,* Raebeck returns to the eastern Long Island of his youth, to the "empty roadways winding through farms and woodlands, open vistas of sea and sky..." (from back cover), and to the embattled people who live there.

As numerous critics have noted, Shelby Raebeck is that rare East End writer who writes from a genuinely local perspective, about the off-season, the underbelly, the people who grind out their daily lives amidst the area's confoundingly beautiful land and seascapes.

Also by Shelby Raebeck

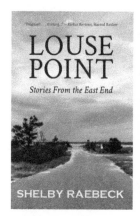

"Poignant...riveting."
Starred Review,
Kirkus Reviews

"Intuitive, thoughtful,
shrewd."
Kirkus Reviews

"Visionary...haunting..."
David Stevenson, author
of *Warnings Against Myself*